# LONE
# STARS

# MIKE LUPICA

SCHOLASTIC INC.

ISBN 978-1-338-33962-8

12 11 10 9 8 7 6 5 4 3 2 1          18 19 20 21 22 23

Printed in the U.S.A.                          40

This edition first printing, September 2018

Edited by Michael Green
Design by Ellice M. Lee
Text set in Life BT

*This book is for my Pop, Bene Lupica,*
*who came home from flying in B-24s*
*over Europe at the age of twenty*
*to live a great American life.*

# ONE

**C**LAY'S COACH SAID YOU CAN'T play football scared. Well, that wasn't exactly the way Coach Monty Cooper— Coach Coop—said it in his South Texas accent. He said you *cain't* play football scared, and to never forget that, because he never had.

Coach Coop said a lot of things, about football and life and Texas, mostly about his playing days with the Dallas Cowboys and how much he missed those days, every single damn one of them. When he'd say that, the last part, he'd apologize for swearing and tell them all over again that they ought to have a swear pot for him. Clay always thought that if they did, they'd be on their way to *buying* the Cowboys.

And Coach Coop had all these expressions, some of them Texas and some of them—at least to Clay's twelve-year-old mind—just plain weird. But they were all just plain Coach, who liked to joke that a lot of people he'd met across the years, from his time playing college ball at TCU and then with the Cowboys, said he acted as if he'd played without a helmet.

"I really should've been born in another time," Coach said

after practice one day to Clay and his buddy David Guerrero, the quarterback for the Alamo Stars.

"What time would that be?" Clay said.

Coach Coop looked at him and said, "Thought I told you never to ask me what time it was." He laughed and turned his head and spit, something he did a lot. "A lot of 'em when I played were smarter than me," he said to Clay and David. "Heck, most of 'em were smarter than me. But not one I ever played with or against was ever any by-God tougher."

He had been born in San Antonio and played his high school ball here before he went to TCU and then to the Cowboys. And because he had finally come back home and was living in San Antonio again, he was always referencing the Alamo when he'd give them a pep talk, telling them that those good ol' boys hadn't gotten beat, that old General Santy Anna—which is what Coach called him—had just been allowed to have way too many men on the field.

But as big as Coach was with all his expressions and all his stories about his playing days, the expression he kept coming back to was the one about not playing scared. He made doing that sound like some kind of sin. Or a crime against football.

Coach Monty Cooper said that once you put on those shoulder pads and strapped on that helmet, you could be a lot of things. Smart or dumb. Fast or slow. Step ahead of the action or step behind.

You just couldn't be afraid.

Not of the other team. Not of making a mistake, or losing.

Especially not afraid of getting hit, of taking a good lick, as Coach liked to say.

And that had never been a problem for Clay Hollis from the first time *he'd* put on pads and strapped on a helmet.

Until today.

# TWO

CLAY WAS A WIDE RECEIVER, the best on the Stars, probably the best in the Pee Wee Division—there wasn't a player on the team who didn't hate that name—of San Antonio Pop Warner, the division for kids between ten and twelve.

In the words of David Guerrero, whose job it was to get the ball to him, when it came to football, Clay Hollis was *serious*.

He wasn't the biggest receiver they had. But he was big enough, with hands and speed to match, and with the gift that Coach Coop said the best receivers had to have: the ability for finding a seam in the defense a couple of steps before it opened up for him. Coach Coop had been a wide receiver at TCU himself, then drafted as one by the Cowboys, even though he'd become more famous later—Clay knew by reading up on him—for being a total maniac on special teams. But he knew that sometimes it took more than speed and good moves to get you open downfield. You just had to be born with the ability to see the field; see things that were about to develop before they actually did; see even the smallest patch of green waiting for you, whether it was in the middle of the field or a place on the sideline, where you'd have enough room to make a catch and keep your feet inbounds.

Sometimes that meant busting a pattern when Clay would look back and see that David Guerrero was scrambling away from a pass rush, something David could do with the best of them.

It was another thing Clay had going for him. He knew where he needed to go when he had to make up a brand-new pass pattern on the fly, like when he and David were playing touch football on the big stretch of lawn behind Clay's house. Clay knew where he needed to be, and David knew where to look for him. From the time they'd first started playing catch together, it was as if they were able to hack into each other's brains, no problem.

But the problem today wasn't fixing a busted pattern. It was a simple crossing pattern over the middle, third and eight, first quarter of a still-scoreless game against the River Walk Lions. That was when Clay got hit, and his day changed, just like that. He loved reading about sports and sports history, not just football, and remembered reading one time about how Mike Tyson, the boxer, said everybody had a plan until they got hit.

Bobby Flores, a friend who'd moved out of the east San Antonio school district last summer, was guarding him. But Clay had made a neat inside move as soon as he'd cleared the line of scrimmage and gotten a step on Bobby. All he needed.

That wasn't Clay's problem, either.

His problem was that David Guerrero, with all the time in the world in the pocket, led Clay by too much with his pass. Not a lot. But it didn't take much to blow up what should have been a simple completion, make what should have been an easy-as-pie completion—and a sure first down—into something harder.

A whole *lot* harder.

Hard, as Clay had heard plenty of times already this season, as his old coach's head.

When the ball was halfway to him, Clay started to think it wasn't just a bit of an overthrow, but might be completely out of his reach. Unacceptable. Totally. You wanted the ball or somebody else wanted it more. That was something else he had heard from Coach Coop plenty of times. So at what he thought was the exact right moment, Clay extended his arms and himself as much as he could, almost as if he were diving for the ball without his feet leaving the ground, just because he thought he might have a better chance of collecting the ball and holding on to it if he didn't have to worry about coughing it up when he hit the ground. Or the ground hit him.

Somehow, he was able to reach the ball.

And he was so happy to have the sweet feel of the ball in his hands, the feel of him pulling it in, that he never saw the safety coming at him from the other direction.

Antrel Vance was the kid's name. Clay remembered him from last season. He was big enough to be a linebacker then, had only gotten bigger in the last year. He was at safety because of how fast he was, fast enough to return kicks, and even play some wide receiver. And even though the ball was clearly out of Antrel's reach now, and he hadn't gotten to it in time to make an interception, he did the next best thing:

Put a lick on Clay and tried to knock the ball out of his hands.

Totally legal. Totally clean hit. No intent to injure. Antrel didn't lead with his helmet, which would have gotten him ejected from the game, same as it would have in high school or college. He didn't come in too high on Clay, or too low, just dropped his shoulder and went plowing into his midsection.

Lot of things seemed to happen at once.

Clay felt all the air come out of him as he started to fall to his left. But he wasn't thinking about that, about air going out but not coming in or the sensation he had that he was flying now. All he was worrying about was holding on to the ball—which he did—even when his left shoulder and elbow and his helmet were hitting the ground at about the exact same moment.

When he did hit, he felt the way you did when you weren't paying attention and picked something up off the kitchen floor and then hit the back of your head on the counter when you straightened back up.

But as much as his head and his elbow hurt, somehow he had the presence of mind to get to his feet as quickly as he could, as if the hit he'd just taken was no big deal, because he knew that if he didn't, his mom would already be moving out of the stands behind Holy Cross High School. She'd done it before. She was one of *those* football moms, watching every move he made like a hawk, especially if she thought he'd taken any kind of shot to his head. And the last thing you wanted if you were a twelve-year-old football player—one who played his home games in the shadow of the Alamo and who prided himself on being as tough as his coach—was to have your mom down on the field seeing if her little boy was all right.

7

When he was halfway up, still holding on to the ball with his left hand, Antrel grabbed his right hand, right before Clay tossed the ball to the ref.

Clay could feel the ringing in his ears. Knew he'd gotten his bell rung good. But he wasn't going to let Antrel know that. Or show him how happy he was to suddenly be able to take a good, deep breath.

"You good?" Antrel said.

"Am I good?" Clay said. "I'm *great,* now that I know that's all you got, dude."

Antrel smiled, as if knowing that if Clay were giving him a little chirp, it meant he was all right.

"Long game," he said. "We'll see about that."

He leaned forward then and they touched helmets, Clay hoping that Antrel didn't have any more hurt in him than that. Antrel or anybody else on the Lions.

Because being in the air that way, not knowing how he was going to land or how hard he was going to land—and then landing as hard as he did—hadn't just knocked the wind out of him. It had scared him.

But he jogged casually back to the huddle while the first-down chains were moved, keeping his head down, but *feeling* his mom's eyes on him. So he gave a quick look up to where he knew she was sitting in the stands. She wasn't sitting. She was standing, staring straight at him.

So he gave her a thumbs-up, hoping that convinced her that he was okay. She nodded and gave him a thumbs-up sign back.

But are you okay? Clay asked himself.

Really?

His head was still ringing. He could still feel the burn in his left elbow. But it was funny. He was more scared of taking himself out of the game than he was about getting hit again the way Antrel had just hit him anytime soon.

Before David told them what the next play was, he turned to Clay and he was the one asking him, "You good?"

"Perfect," Clay said.

Most of Clay's reading was about wide receivers. Around the time of the NFL draft, he liked to read up on the top wide receivers coming out of college, and learn how all the so-called draft experts were evaluating them. And when he did, the two biggest negatives were always the same:

They talked about guys who would "short arm" receptions, or possible receptions, in traffic. It meant they'd pull up in traffic, or wouldn't lay out the way Clay just had, because they were afraid of getting popped the way Antrel popped Clay.

That was one negative.

The other was when they'd talk about a receiver who came out of the game if he did get popped.

Clay had never been one of those guys and wasn't going to be one today. He wasn't going to sit out a single play. He was going to stay out there.

David targeted him three more times the rest of the half, *only* three more times because the Stars were having so much success running the ball. As much as Coach Coop loved throwing the ball, there was no reason to do that right now against the Lions the way they were moving the chains by keeping it on the ground.

"You know why those TV ratings for the NFL are a rocket to the moon?" he told the team before the season, when he explained that they were going to be what he called the "throwing-est" team in the league. "Because the ball's always in the air, is why."

Clay caught two of the balls David threw him, even though he nearly dropped one in the flat, wide-open as he was, because at the very last second he looked to see where the outside linebacker was. The third ball was thrown wild, way over his head, because David was being chased. He had to get rid of the ball too soon as Clay got behind Bobby Flores and Antrel, who'd been late getting over to help out once Clay was behind Bobby.

The game was 13–6, Stars, at the half and was still 13–6 late in the third quarter when the Stars were driving again, David still content to be handing the ball off, mostly to their best running back, Josh Bodeen. Clay kept waiting for the Lions to put more guys in the box as a way of jamming up Josh. But they didn't do that until the Stars had crossed into their territory. They brought up all their linebackers and even one of their other safeties sometimes, leaving an awful lot of the middle of the field for Antrel to cover. They'd only been playing against Antrel Vance for a couple of years now, but Clay had used another one of Coach Coop's expressions at halftime and told David that Antrel could still cover all of the earth that water didn't.

Now they stuffed Josh for no gain on first down. David pitched it to him on second down, but Antrel was blitzing and dropped Josh for a two-yard loss. Third and twelve, Lions' forty-two-yard line, minute left in the quarter. Chance for the Stars, if they could keep driving, to make it a two-score game. And the way the Stars' defense had been playing all day long, their madman middle linebacker, Bryce Darrell, leading the charge, Clay was pretty confident that a two-touchdown lead was going to be more than enough to get them to 2–0 for the season.

David told them the play that Coach had just sent in, one that even had Clay's number attached to it:

"Eighty-Seven post."

He wore 87 because, as much as he loved him his Dallas Cowboys, as much as he loved watching Dez Bryant catch balls when he was behaving himself, his favorite receiver was Jordy Nelson of the Packers. Clay liked to think that he and David Guerrero were as connected on a football field as Aaron Rodgers and Jordy were.

Eighty-Seven post was the same play, over the middle, they'd run in the first quarter before Antrel had put him down and he'd hit his head, even though he was the only one at Holy Cross High School who knew how hard.

"This time I'll lead you the way I'm supposed to," David said to him in a quiet voice as they broke the huddle.

"Please," Clay said. "I'll pay you."

He heard David laugh. But Clay meant it. He told himself that he wasn't afraid to go back into traffic, that if you were a wide receiver that was part of the job: playing in traffic. Told himself that the nerves he was feeling as he took his position were the good kind of nerves, the ones that you were supposed to use to your advantage in sports, the kind that made you focus even harder.

What he was really telling himself was not to be the short-arm guy. Be the guy you've always been, the one who makes the tough catch. One hard hit wasn't going to stop him from being that guy.

Was it?

He put a different move on Bobby Flores this time, gave him a quick little lean to the outside, putting a head fake with it, like he was going to break for the sideline. Then he planted his left foot and made one of those clean cuts on which he prided himself. As soon as he did, he felt as if he were running free, not just a little open field in front of him.

A lot.

Then the little alarm that would go off in his head went off now, telling him it was time to turn back for the ball, to see if it was already on its way. It worked like that a lot with him and David, their timing was already that good, more often than not he would have released the ball *after* Clay made his move, but *before* his head was turned around.

There it was, already on its way, one of David's tight little spirals. In addition to all the other things that made him a good receiver, Clay had been blessed with great vision. David told him one time that if Clay had to, he could read what was written on the side of a football like he was reading a chart at the eye doctor's office.

He was already thinking about more than just making a catch, getting his team a first down. He was thinking about making a big run, maybe all the way to the house.

*Don't get ahead of yourself.*

*First make the catch,* then *run with it.*

It was then that he heard somebody yell, "Look out!"

He knew it happened all the time in the secondary, even in

Pop Warner ball, guys trying to distract you. Some were cheesy enough to yell, "Drop it!" when you were wide open, trying to break your concentration just enough to actually turn a catch into a drop. The only way to stop them was by making the catch, showing them it didn't work.

But sometimes it was one of your own guys, trying to give you a heads-up that there was trouble heading your way.

Clay would never know who had done the yelling. But just as the ball was about to arrive—right on the money, as David had promised—Clay looked to see where Antrel was.

And even though Antrel wasn't right on top of him like the last time he'd run 87 post, he was close enough.

Clay slowed down. Not a lot. Just enough. What should have been a perfect, right-in-stride catch, what *might* have been a catch and run if he could have put a good enough move on Antrel, became an incompletion instead, the ball sailing between Clay's hands and Antrel's. It might have looked like an overthrow. Clay knew better. And felt sick.

He ran off the field, head down, as the guys on the punt team passed him. Clay walked to the end of the bench, where he'd left his water bottle, taking a long swallow because suddenly his throat felt drier than dirt.

When he finished and tossed the bottle back under the bench, David Guerrero was standing there.

"What the heck, dude?" he said. "Why the darn heck did you pull up like that?"

"I didn't," Clay said, and felt a little sicker.

"I know you better than anybody," David said, trying to keep his voice down. "Sometimes I think I know you better than you know yourself. So don't tell me what I just saw, and what we both knew you did."

Clay didn't get a chance to answer, didn't have to decide whether or not to lie to his best friend's face again, because now this huge cheer went up on the Stars' sideline. Clay turned to see what had happened and saw Bryce Darrell, his helmet turned sideways on his head, showing his teammates the ball, meaning he'd just separated the Lions' punt returner from it.

"What happened?" Clay asked Josh Bodeen, who was standing in front of him.

"Kid should have made a fair catch," Josh said. "Or just let the ball bounce. But he didn't. And Bryce just ran right through the play. And him."

"Yeah," David said, tossing his own water bottle and getting ready to get back out there with the offense. "Just like you're supposed to in football."

Stars' ball, fifteen-yard line. Josh lost a yard on first down. On second, Coach Coop sent in another play for Clay, a fade to the corner of the end zone.

"The ball will be there," David said.

"So will I," Clay said.

"I know that, too," David said.

It was their favorite pattern because this one really was all timing, with no real threat of the ball being intercepted unless David underthrew it, and badly. And Clay knew *that* wasn't happening, not with an even better chance to put the game away. Clay knew that if he was covered closely enough by Bobby Flores, and even if Antrel came over to double-team him, David was throwing the ball into the parking lot.

Clay wasn't covered. This time he faked to the inside, as if he were going back to the middle of the field one more time. This time, after leaning left, he pushed off with his right foot, to the outside. Once again he got a step on Bobby, giving himself all the room he needed, the only thing closing on him now the back line of the end zone. He looked over his shoulder to see the ball floating over Bobby's head, looked the ball right into his hand. As he caught it, he quickly checked to make sure his two feet were inbounds. They were.

Now when he looked back, he saw the ref's hands in the air, signaling touchdown. Clay ran over and handed him the ball, the way he always did. As soon as he did, David came running over to him, and they did the little jump-in they did after a score.

"More like it," David said.

"Owed you one," Clay said.

"Nah," David said. "Maybe you owed yourself one."

They didn't get the conversion, Josh getting stopped on the one. So it was still 19–6, Stars, the way it ended.

Clay was standing next to Coach Coop when the last desperation heave from the Lions' quarterback sailed out of bounds.

"Well, Coach," Clay said, trying to sound like him. "That there was a good 'un."

Coach looked down, put his hand out so Clay could give him a high five. "Three in a row is what it is."

Clay grinned. "I know it might have felt like we were in two games today," he said. "But we're only two and oh."

"There I go, gettin' ahead of my old self," he said. Then he gave Clay a long look and said, "How's the head?"

"Hard," Clay said.

Then he watched his coach limp toward the middle of the field to shake hands with the Lions' coach, on knees that had undergone so many surgeries that Coach Monty Cooper said he'd righteously lost count of them. His doctor kept telling him that he'd be better off with a cane. Coach kept telling the doctor, one day. Just not any day soon.

There was going to be a big celebration at the Cowboys' stadium, AT&T Stadium, on Thanksgiving, honoring the Cowboys' last Super Bowl team. It was the team's annual Thanksgiving Day game, and there was no way he was ever going to be on that field, and hearing the cheers again, and there was no way he was going to walk out there using a stick, looking like some frail old man.

Clay asked him one time when it was just the two of them if it was worth it, all the hits he had taken, and not just to his knees.

"Ever' one," Coach said.

And I'm worried about one hit, Clay thought to himself as he watched his coach.

Suck it up, Alamo Boy.

# THREE

CLAY ACTUALLY THOUGHT HIS MOM might love football more than his dad did.

His dad had been a decent running back at Holy Cross High, just not good enough to get the college scholarship offer that some of his teammates had, not even from one of the smaller Texas schools. Ben Hollis tried to make a joke out of it now, about how he couldn't get past the bias college recruiters had against running backs who weren't fast enough, strong enough, or shifty enough. But Clay could tell it still bothered him that he never got the chance to keep going.

"Those Friday Night Lights turned out to be as bright as they ever got for your dad," Ben Hollis said.

But he still loved his football. He'd gone to the University of Texas, met Katherine Green there, fell in love with her, finally married her while he was still attending law school at UT. He still loved his Longhorns football, which was like a religion in their family, and the Cowboys, and served on the board for Pop Warner football in San Antonio.

But Clay really did believe his mom loved football more. She'd grown up in Austin, in the shadow of UT. Her two older brothers, Clay's uncles, had both been linebackers for the Longhorns. The four season tickets to UT games that had been in the family from the time she was a little girl had been given to her when Clay's grandfather had passed. They no longer made the ninety-minute drive to Austin for home games now that Clay had Pop Warner games on Saturday mornings or Saturday afternoons. But they still managed to see three or four games a season, and never missed one on Saturday night.

It was because Clay's mom loved football as much as she did, and had grown up in it, that she hated having to embrace what she called the "new information" about how dangerous the game could be, even at the Pop Warner level. And why she asked him after every practice and every game if he'd taken any hits to the head, and not to lie to her.

Even if she was at the game, he knew what the first question was going to be when it was over:

"How's the noggin?"

When she asked today, Clay tried to make a joke out of it.

"Have I met you, ma'am?" he said to her.

"Not funny."

"*Kind* of funny," he said.

"Just being a mom," she said. "A modern football mom."

"The worst . . . I mean, the *best* kind!"

"Still not funny," she said. "Like it wasn't funny when you got cleaned out the way you did going across the middle."

"You mean that play where I took a good, clean hit and held on?"

"You were slow getting up."

"Was not."

"Was too," she said. "I thought you'd figured out by now that moms know everything."

Clay grinned at her. "Wait! You know what it feels like to go across the middle with a cornerback riding you your hip and a safety coming up on you and filled with bad intentions?"

"Oh, here we go," she said. "I can't *really* understand football because I never played the game."

"Well, you said it."

"Let's go have lunch," she said. "On the way home, I'll try to figure out who's the better lawyer in the family, you or your father."

Ben Hollis had been listening to the back-and-forth between them, smiling. But now he said, "Wait a second. I feel like I just got hit!"

They drove home. Clay took off his football pants and cleats and T-shirt he wore underneath his jersey, and took a shower. His dad didn't stick around for lunch, saying that he had a golf date, but would be home in plenty of time for dinner and to watch the Longhorns play Oklahoma State in Stillwater later. So it was just Clay and his mom at lunch, going over the game, his mom once again impressing him with the things she picked up on, making him think all over again that there couldn't possibly be a football mom in San Antonio, or maybe the world, who saw the things she saw, who could do a better job of breaking down a game, whether it was the Stars or the Longhorns or the Cowboys.

More and more, though, she wanted to talk about concussions, wanted to make sure that Pop Warner and Coach Coop and Clay himself were doing everything possible to protect his extremely valuable, practically priceless brain.

"I was reading this piece yesterday," she said now, "about how dangerous a head injury can be to a small child." She smiled across the table. "Maybe I should have Antrel read it."

"Mom," Clay said, "I'm *twelve*. If that lick Antrel put on me is the worst one I get all year, I'm gonna be fine."

"So you admit it was a harder hit than usual?"

"He knocked the breath out of me," he said. "You're acting as if he knocked my helmet clear off."

"Your helmet hit the ground."

"Don't you hate when that happens, the ground sneaking up on you that way in a sport where they get to tackle you?"

"Clay Hollis," she said. "I am just trying to educate you in real time, at the *same* time I'm educating myself."

"I know that. And we both know that if you see *Concussion* one more time, you're going to have that sucker memorized."

It was the Will Smith movie about CTE, the condition caused by repeated hits to the head, the one discovered by the doctor Will Smith played.

"I'm not one of those moms they talk about who's trying to kill football," she said. "You know how much I love football. I'm just looking to do all the right things to protect my one and only baby boy."

"Just don't treat me like a baby," he said. "And stop trying to scare me with all this new information of yours."

"Ours," she said.

"Could I have more coleslaw please?"

"Sounds like somebody wants to change the subject."

"Only 'cause I do."

She spooned more of her homemade slaw on his plate and said, "You have any plans for this afternoon?"

"Same old, same old," he said. "Watch guys try to knock each other's brains out in college football."

She closed her eyes and slowly shook her head. "Sigh," she said. When she opened her eyes, she said to Clay, "You know I'm not trying to scare you, because I know what your coach says."

They recited it together, like they were in class.

"You . . . cain't . . . play . . . scared."

And laughed.

"You think Coach is moving even slower than he was when we started practice?" he said.

"He just looks the same to me," she said. "Older than he really is."

"All he talks about is sprinting out on that field at Thanksgiving, no matter how bad his knees hurt," Clay said. "Says one last time, he's gonna be that wild man who used to come charging out of the tunnel at Texas Stadium the same way."

"I wonder sometimes," Katherine Hollis said, "if he remembers those days being a whole lot better than they really were."

Clay reminded his mom of one more thing Coach liked to say, how he figured he was ahead of the game because he could still remember them at all.


David called after lunch and said he'd be right over, as soon as he cleaned his room.

He lived only three blocks away, but Clay knew what his room usually looked like.

"Half an hour?" Clay said.

David told him to hold on and texted him a picture of his bedroom.

"I feel you," Clay said. "See you in an hour."

Clay pointed the remote at the small TV set next to his desk, channel-surfed through a bunch of games until he found one he was interested in, Navy at Notre Dame.

But it wasn't the game he was focused on, because he kept replaying his own game inside his head, which had finally stopped hurting, not that he was going to tell his mom that, or anybody else. Including David.

He told himself to stop worrying about one hit and one dropped pass. He'd told his mom that he hoped that Antrel's hit was the worst one he got all season. Same with that short-armed ball. If that was the worst play he made all season, well, then it was probably going to be a great season.

But he couldn't let go of either one. Was he afraid of his next hard hit or just afraid of *being* afraid? Maybe one of these days, in a nice way, he was going to have to ask his mom to stop talking about his brain, because it was hurting his head.

You know what this new information really was?

It was TMI.

Too *much* information.

When David finally arrived on his bike and asked what Clay wanted to do, Clay said, "Play catch."

"But we just finished playing a *game*."

"Whoa," Clay said. "Name another time in your life when you didn't want to throw a football around with me."

"Can't we just veg and watch guys do that on that great big TV in your rec room?"

"No."

"I should have asked what you wanted to do before I came over," he said.

"You know you would have come anyway," Clay said. "Remember something: I know you as well as you know me."

"I give," David said, and grinned.

He was just a little taller than Clay and outweighed him by maybe ten pounds, if that. But you could see already that he had the arm of a high school QB. Their plan was to play high school ball together someday at Holy Cross, the way both their dads had, then continue having their game of catch at the University of Texas. It was part plan and part dream. Maybe more dream.

Clay got his football out of his closet, David took it out of his hands, they walked down the stairs and out the back door toward the back lawn, one that seemed to stretch out ahead of them the way the rest of Saturday afternoon did.

As soon as his feet were on the grass, Clay took off, at full speed, running in the direction of the tree line in the distance, feeling a slight breeze in his face, turning back at the same moment David yelled, "Ball!" He looked up then, saw the ball outlined against the blue sky, thinking this might be another time when David might have led him too much, but knowing he'd run all the way to the San Antonio River if it meant running it down.

The ball was two strides too far, but at the last possible second,

Clay dove, like it was a racing dive in a swimming pool, and caught the ball maybe a foot before it hit the grass, and right before he did.

Man, he loved football. He knew just about every boy his age in Texas loved it, too. Just not more than he did. And if getting hit, and hitting the ground the way he just did, was a part of it, he was cool with that. Totally.

Put him down, he was getting right back up, the way Coach always had.

"He's back!" David yelled at him.

"Yeah," Clay yelled back. "And he ain't going anywhere."

When Clay was back with him, David said, "Hey? I'm sorry I said what I said about you pulling up on that one ball."

"You were right to say what you did," Clay said. "And just so you know, dog? It won't happen again."

"Didn't think so," David said. "Now stop running your mouth and run out for another pass."

Clay did. Somehow the breeze felt as if it were at his back now. And that nothing could catch him. Or bring him down.

# FOUR

I T WAS AFTER PRACTICE ON Tuesday night that Coach pulled Clay aside. Most of his teammates were already headed for the parking lot by then, where Clay's mom was waiting for him. But Coach said what he wanted to say wouldn't take long.

"Now, I might act as though I miss stuff sometimes," he said. "Some days I feel like a real broken-down cowboy, instead of a guy who played for the Cowboys."

"No way," Clay said. "You could probably get to the outside and block a punt next Sunday if they needed you to."

Coach Coop stared down at Clay, who'd always thought that the lines in Coach's face did make him look a little bit like a cowboy out of some old movie. And Clay's mom was right: He did look older than he really was. And even more tired sometimes.

Except when he smiled. And he smiled now. And looked like pictures of him you could find on the Internet from when he was young.

"You're a good 'un," he said to Clay. "What were we talkin' about?"

"About how people think you miss stuff, even though I don't."

Coach nodded, as if he'd found his place in a book he was reading.

"I know that safety of theirs put a hurting on you the other day," he said. "And if you hadn't gotten up right away, liken you did, I would've gotten out there like my knees weren't all shot to hell and back."

"But I did get up quick."

"That you did." Coach nodded again. "But then later, I saw you not run through that ball."

So he didn't miss much, not that he had to prove it to Clay. "Sorry, Coach," he said.

"Don't be sorry," Coach said. "All that means is that you're human."

"But you always say—"

"I know what I always say," he said, cutting Clay off. "Least some of the time I know. But that's not the point of what we're talking about right here. The point is, I saw what you did and you know what you did. And if I'd seen it happen again, I would've had you stand next to me for a spell and watch a little bit until you were ready to go back out there. But it didn't happen again. And then you made us a play later, didn't you?"

"If I'd dropped that ball," Clay said, "I would've taken myself out of the game."

"Stuck your head right back in there, too."

"Well, not exactly, Coach. It *was* a fade pattern. I didn't have to worry much about the end line smacking me upside my head."

Coach smiled again. "Course it was a fade," he said. "But the important thing was, you made the catch."

Clay told him he sure had, as the two of them began walking toward the parking lot, where his mom was still waiting, and where Coach's pickup was parked.

"I won't let you down, Coach," Clay said. "I promise."

In his mind, it would be tougher letting down the toughest guy he knew than letting himself down. Because one thing was sure:

Monty Cooper had never been afraid to take a hit.

But Clay was, just four days later.

# FIVE

I T HAPPENED AT THE STARS' next game, against the Vikings, on the same field behind Holy Cross, just because the Vikings used it as their home field, too.

And it wasn't just the same field as last Saturday, it was almost in the same exact part of it, on the same pass pattern on which Clay had flinched against the Lions. And this time it happened in the fourth quarter, Stars behind 13–12, just over two minutes left.

It was only the third game of the season, but this was Clay's best so far, no lie, and no fear. He was up against another terrific cover guy, Henry Morales, who was as fast as Clay was, who trusted his own speed enough to crowd Clay at the line of scrimmage and not worry about Clay getting behind him and beating him deep. Sometimes he was close enough to Clay when the ball was snapped that he could have reached across and shaken Clay's hand.

But Clay had gotten Henry more than Henry had gotten him, scoring two touchdowns, making a couple of tough catches— back to being his specialty again today—in traffic. Now the Stars were driving, trying to get a game off one of the best teams in their league. Before the drive had started, Coach Coop, who called the plays, told Clay to strap on his helmet real tight because they were going to feed him the ball like he was a hot shooter in basketball.

"Don't worry," Clay said. "I'll be open."

The Stars had gotten the ball back from the Vikings with four minutes left. Half of that was gone. The ball was on the Vikings' thirty-yard line. Clay had already caught three balls on the drive, two on the sideline to save time on the clock, one a little slant, left to right, that gave Clay room to run before Henry brought him down from behind, but not before another Stars' first down. The Vikings' middle linebacker, Tayshawn Moore, got a piece of the tackle, too, as he tried to knock the ball loose from Clay and ended up putting his helmet into Clay's right hip instead, catching it just right. Major stinger.

But Clay didn't show the other team anything and popped right up. Never let them know how good they got you, even when they did get you good. His hip felt a little bit the way your elbow did after you landed on what his mom had always called his "funny bone." But Clay made sure not to limp, not even a little bit, as he jogged back to the huddle, and then caught a break, just in case Coach was going to have David throw it to him again.

Coach called one of the two timeouts he had left. So Clay got a chance—casually—to walk it off while Maddie, David's sister and the team manager, came running out with water.

Clay walked around behind the huddle, as if he just couldn't wait for the next snap. What he was really doing was trying to take some of the sting out of his hip.

"You want some water, Number Eighty-Seven?" Maddie said

to him, smiling, kneeling in the middle of the huddle. "Don't make me come over there."

"I'm good," he said.

Maddie knew her football. Clay's mom said she was the same kind of football girl she'd been when she was Maddie's age.

"You sure?" she said. "Pretty hot out here."

"I hadn't noticed."

Keep moving, he told himself.

"Very funny," she said. He saw her staring at him. "You sure you're okay?"

"Gorgeous."

"You wish."

When David came back to the huddle after talking to Coach, he gave Clay a soft rap on his helmet with his knuckle before he said, "Deep curl." It was one of their favorites. Clay was supposed to take off as if he were running a fly pattern, then plant, come back for the ball, which sometimes would be right on top of him if David had timed things out right.

"I'm gonna lock my eyes on Will until the last second," David said, meaning Will Kellerman, their other wide receiver. "Then I'm gonna turn and put one on your numbers."

"Love it," Clay said, hoping he had his usual burst when he came off the line, because he was still feeling as if somebody had hit him on the bone of his hip with a piece of wood.

He didn't need a great burst because he wasn't going deep. He just needed good. And got it. And when he did come to a stop and started coming back for the ball, Henry wasn't close to him, because Clay had suckered him into thinking he *was* going deep.

There was just one problem.

A couple, actually.

One was that David's pass was off target, off to Clay's right, toward the middle of the field. Not out of his reach. But he was going to have to go get it.

The other was that David had been totally suckered by Tayshawn, who was shading Will, double-teaming him, acting as if he were following David's eyes. But as soon as David made his turn, squared his shoulders toward Clay, and rushed the throw just enough to float the ball toward the middle, Tayshawn was coming full speed at Clay, and the ball.

Or both.

The Vikings didn't wear purple, the way the Vikings of the NFL did. Their jerseys were bright red. As Clay turned to his right to reach for the ball, he saw all this red in front of him, like some fireball heading his way.

His first mistake was taking his eyes off the ball. His second, which turned out to be much worse, was shying away from Tayshawn Moore.

He still could have made the catch if he'd kept running at the ball in a straight line, if he'd ended up where he was supposed to be. But he didn't.

It was why it turned out to be Tayshawn Moore who caught the ball in stride; it was Tayshawn who broke into the clear, running the other way, toward the Stars' end zone.

Clay chased him, he did, because he knew it was the whole game that was running away from him. But he felt like a dog chasing a fast car. No hurt in his right hip or leg now. Just a much bigger hurt in the pit of his stomach, trying to burn a hole in it.

Clay finally gave up at about the twenty-yard line, watched Tayshawn cross the goal line, then waited for the ref who'd also been chasing the play to catch up, so Tayshawn could hand him the ball. Tayshawn was cool. He didn't celebrate or do anything to show up the Stars, just ran toward the Vikings' sideline before most of his teammates surrounded him.

All Clay could do was stand there, turn, and look at the scoreboard behind the end zone, watch as "13" for the Vikings became "19." When their quarterback made a sweet fake and then kept the ball for the conversion, it was 20–12, Vikings. It was the way the game ended.

But Clay knew it had really ended when he went one way, the wrong way, and the ball went another.

First loss of the season.

Big 'un.

# SIX

**T**HEY ALWAYS TOLD YOU IN sports that nobody really remembered why you lost, just that you lost. But every time Clay would hear that he'd think, well, yeah, tell that to Russell Wilson and the Seahawks about the time they lost the Super Bowl to the Patriots because Wilson threw an interception on the one-yard line. Tell that to the Falcons after they blew a twenty-five-point lead against the Patriots in the Super Bowl two years later.

Clay knew why the Stars had lost.

They had lost because of *him*.

That interception wasn't on David.

It was on *him*.

They'd lost because he'd been afraid to stick his head in there, been afraid of contact in a contact sport, and that's why Tayshawn had ended up with a ball that should have been his.

And if only David and Coach had noticed what happened in the last game when Clay pulled up short and came up short, anybody who knew anything about football could see plain as day what had happened today. With the game on the line and the ball in the air, he'd flat chickened out. Hundred percent. Or hundred and ten percent, another thing they liked to say in sports.

Coach didn't mention the pick six when he briefly spoke to the team after the game. No need to, Clay thought. Coach didn't need to draw them a picture. He just told them it was one loss in a long season, that there were plenty of Saturdays left, to learn from what had happened and build on it.

"Think about it a little, think about what all of us could've done better, and then just throw it out like trash," he said, before telling them all he'd see them at practice on Tuesday night.

Clay hadn't said a word to his teammates on the Stars' last drive after Tayshawn's touchdown. He hadn't said a word to David since the game ended, even knowing he couldn't avoid him much longer since Clay's mom and dad were giving David, whose parents were away for the weekend, a ride home.

Finally, Clay sat down next to David at the end of their bench. David had already taken off his helmet and jersey and pads, was down to a gray T-shirt that was so wet with sweat it looked as if he'd gone swimming in it. Now Clay pulled his jersey over his head and took off his pads.

"Before you say something, let me say something," Clay said.

"Wasn't gonna say something."

"But you're thinking it."

It got a small grin out of David Guerrero, a small shake of the head. "You don't want to know what I'm thinking."

Clay took a deep breath, let it out. "I know what I did."

"Think I don't?" David said.

"And there's nothing you could say about it, whether you do or don't, that could make me feel any worse than I already do."

"How about better?"

"Not happening," Clay said. "I bailed out, is what I did. Didn't know I was going to until I did, or that the worst thing that could possibly happen on that play was about to happen. I kept my head in there all day." He closed his eyes, but not for long, because as soon as he did, he could see Tayshawn's number 56 as he ran down the field. "Kept my head in there until I didn't."

"I know what it's like," David said.

"No," Clay said, "you don't."

"Not from football," David said. "Baseball. I almost quit baseball this year."

"You never told me that."

"I never told anybody," David said. "But there was a time after Bobby Lopez hit me with that pitch in the middle of the season that I felt myself flinching anytime a ball would come inside."

"I never noticed."

"'Cause I fought through it," David said. "Same as you will."

"Told you not to try to make me feel better," Clay said. "I don't deserve that."

"I'm just doing what friends are supposed to do. Telling you the truth."

David scooped up his helmet and jersey and pads into his arms. "Now let's get out of here," he said. "I don't even like football right now."

"My dad," Clay said, "says that's against the law in Texas."

"Just in Texas?" David said, and they both laughed.

Even though he didn't want to feel better, Clay was starting to. Not a lot. A little. It was all because of the guy who Clay had let down more than anybody on their team today.

He hadn't been there for David. But now David was there for him. Clay guessed that was about as good a definition of friendship as any.

If Clay could have managed it, he would have avoided the subject of the Stars-Vikings game—or at least talking about it—for the rest of the day and night. His mom knew enough to leave it alone after they'd dropped off David and Maddie. All his dad said when the three of them were alone in the car was this:

"Tough one, kid."

Before Clay could respond, his mom, whom he knew would do anything to lighten the mood in the car, quickly turned toward her husband, who was driving, and said, "Gee, you *think*, Sherlock Holmes?"

Clay made himself laugh along with them. He'd asked David if he wanted to come over, just because he thought he should ask, as much as he wanted to be alone. But David said his grandparents were visiting.

It wasn't until they got to the house that Clay's mom reminded him that this was one of the Saturday nights when they'd invited Coach Monty Cooper over for dinner. He'd completely forgotten.

But now it was official that he couldn't leave the game at Holy Cross High, that it had followed him all the way home and was going to follow him all the way to Saturday night, where a few hours later Coach was saying, "You just gotta make yourself do what I did when I played with a game like this one."

"You said throw it in the trash before," Clay reminded him.

"Well," Coach said, "I was about to say it again."

Clay said, "It's hard."

They had finished dinner by now and were sitting in the living room. Coach slapped the arm of his chair and said, "Hell's bells, son. Whoever said sports was gonna be easy? What would be the fun in that?"

The Texas Tech–TCU game was on the television set, but Clay's dad had muted the sound. But every once in a while Clay would look over to check the score, or his eyes would fix on a pass play. Hey, he thought. It's football and it's on TV. He felt obliged to watch.

The adults were having coffee. As always when Coach came to dinner, he seemed in no rush to leave.

Clay knew that he had been divorced at least twice and had one grown daughter, who was living with her husband and their three-year-old son. Coach didn't talk about his daughter very much. In fact, Clay didn't even know her name, but he remembered Coach mentioning at another dinner at the house one time that he'd only seen his grandson once since he'd been born. When he'd said that, Clay wondered what it would be like to never see his own parents or not have them in his life. All Coach said that time about his daughter, before he stopped talking about her, was this:

"She's just part of the dues I'm still payin' for having football be the only family that ever mattered to me."

Monty Cooper had moved home to San Antonio to become a receivers coach at UT–San Antonio. Clay knew this was after he had knocked around for years as an assistant coach, first with the Cowboys, then in college, even one junior college. "It was," Ben Hollis said to Clay's mom one time, "like even his football world kept getting smaller." He never lasted long in one place, even if he did stay at UT–San Antonio for two seasons.

He didn't get another college job after that. He stayed home, saying that San Antonio had always represented the best of him, and not just because of the Alamo, where he said those boys showed you something that everybody should always remember, every time they did remember the Alamo:

That you could be a hero even when you lost.

So he was back home now, even though Clay overheard his parents talking one night after Coach had left their house, and his dad saying that he was back in San Antonio because he didn't have anywhere else to go.

It had been Ben Hollis who'd gone to Monty Cooper and asked him if he'd be willing to coach Pop Warner, that it would mean so much to the league and so much to the kids. And it had been Clay's mom who had started inviting him over for dinner, because of how lonely she felt he was.

"He needs more in his life than all his stories about the old days," is the way she explained it to Clay.

"You make him sound like some kind of sad old man," Clay said, feeling as if he had to defend his coach. "And he's way more than that."

"I'm not saying that at all," she'd said. "I know how you look up to him, and nobody you'd ever look up to could ever be sad in my eyes. It's like he says: There's all kinds of heroes."

"He seems happy enough to me," Clay had said.

"But mostly with his memories."

"Is there something wrong with that?"

"The thing about memories," his mom had said, "is that you want to keep making more. That's what I'm hoping happens this season."

But memories were what Coach Coop was sharing with them now in the living room, about what it was like to play for the Cowboys when they were still on top of the world, back when people used to say that the reason they had to build that famous hole in the roof at old Texas Stadium was so God Himself could watch His Cowboys play.

He talked about how crazy some of his ex-teammates were, how it seemed like when the game was over the new competition was to see how they could out-crazy one another, and sometimes out-party one another. He talked about how the owner, Jerry Jones, wanted to be as much of a star as any of the players with that star on their helmets. He talked about what it was like when people called the Cowboys "America's Team" and really meant it, not like it was now, when even that nickname felt like it was something out of the past.

Coach Coop smiled then and said, "Sort of like me."

But Clay didn't think it was the kind of smile you'd see on Coach's face when Clay or one of his teammates would make a good play.

Clay didn't know how much his parents liked hearing these stories, some of which they'd all heard before, even though Coach always told them like it was the first time.

"We partied hard," Coach said. He looked at Clay and pointed a crooked finger—crooked because he said he broke it so many times—and said, "Even though partying is something I never want you to do, son."

"Bless you," Katherine Hollis said, smiling herself.

"But as hard as we did party," Coach said, "me and those boys played even harder."

Then he was telling about a playoff game Clay had heard him talk about before, that game before his blocked punt against the Packers helped put the Cowboys into their last Super Bowl, the Cowboys team that would be honored on Thanksgiving Day.

"Everybody knew I was on my last legs by then," he said, "and that Coach Switzer was pretty much carrying me when he could have had a younger player in my place because he liked me so much and trusted me not to make mistakes. But even then, I was about to catch that touchdown pass to win the game before that guy on the Eagles knocked me out cold."

Clay, who knew Cowboys history even better than he knew American history, realized right away that Coach was confusing two different games. The Cowboys *had* played their division play-off game against the Eagles that year. But the catch Coach was talking about, the one where he really did get knocked out on the field, had come against the Giants in the Cowboys' second-to-last regular-season game.

Clay knew the play because the first time Coach told him the story about it, Clay had gone to YouTube and looked it up. He wished he'd remembered the way Coach hadn't been afraid to keep *his* head in there better than he had against the Vikings today.

"You mean the Giants game, right, Coach?" Clay said. "Not the Eagles game before you played the Packers in the NFC Championship game?"

Coach looked at Clay, then laughed and slapped his knee, even though Clay noticed that he winced as he did. "There I go," he said, "misremembering again! Course it was the hated Giants."

He looked over at Clay's parents and said, "Look at this little sonofagun. He knows my career better than I do!"

"He knows his Cowboys football, that's for sure," Clay's mom said. "Sometimes I wish he'd study as hard at school as he does about those teams you played on."

Coach Coop said, "You want to hear another good one about that day I probably never told you about?"

Clay felt himself smiling now, thinking that the chances were pretty good that he *had* heard whatever story Coach was about to tell before.

"When I got back to our hotel that night," Coach said, "I'm still feelin' a little fuzzy when I get into the elevator. And when it comes time to push the button for my floor, I can't remember which one to push, 'cause I can't remember what my room number is. I gotta go back to the front desk and ask 'em! Is that the funniest thing you ever heard in your life?"

Clay was watching his mom's face. He knew by now that she didn't think stories like this were ever funny. But she loved Coach Coop. So she didn't say anything. Neither did his dad. Neither did Clay. He looked back at Coach Coop, who was sitting there now, staring over at the football game at the television. Or maybe staring all the way back to that day against the Giants.

"Where was I?" Coach said finally.

Katherine Hollis, who was also pretty good on her Cowboys history, said, "1995."

Coach said, "Wasn't I, though?"

He put his arms on the sides of his chair and pushed himself up and out of it now, wincing even more when his knees took on all his weight. Clay could see the effort it took just to do something as simple as getting out of a chair. Coach thanked Clay's mom again for a delicious dinner, kissed her on the cheek, shook hands with Clay's dad, reached down, and squeezed Clay's shoulder as he told him to stay put.

"I know you feel bad about today," Coach said. "But always remember something: Even bad memories in this game are better than none. 'Cause that means you were out there. That means you were in the game."

Then he told Clay he'd see him at practice, and show himself out. When he got to the door, he turned around, smiled one last time, and said, "How 'bout them Cowboys?"

# SEVEN

**C**LAY LOVED GOING TO THE Alamo.

Some people in San Antonio took it for granted, the way they took the River Walk downtown for granted, like those were just things for tourists to see.

Clay never took the Alamo for granted.

His mom did like to joke that she wished he studied history in school the way he studied football history. But she knew better when it came to the history of the Alamo, which Clay felt he knew as much about as any boy or girl his age in the city. And he never got tired of visiting the old mission that turned into the most famous fortress the state of Texas had ever known, and what his dad just called "the shrine." Every time he did, he felt like he'd gotten into a time machine and traveled back to 1836.

When he was smaller, his parents used to take him over to the Alamo, usually on Sundays after church. But now they felt he was old enough that they could drop him off and pick him up in an hour or two or however long Clay wanted to stay. Today they went to church early, and Clay's dad dropped him off at ten thirty, said he'd be back in a couple of hours so they'd be home in time for the one o'clock football games, even though the Cowboys weren't playing until four fifteen.

"You think Davy Crockett and Jim Bowie and Colonel Travis will make you feel better?" Ben Hollis said.

They both knew he was talking about yesterday's game.

"They always do," Clay said, before adding, "win or lose."

"You know what I always think about those old boys?" Clay's dad said. "That they're the best example ever of how there's all different kinds of way to be winners in this world."

"And heroes."

"Yeah," his dad said. "That, too."

Clay saw that there was a surprisingly good crowd for a Sunday morning once he got inside. He didn't know for sure if a lot of the people were here from out of town. But he always just assumed they were as they moved from point to point, posing for pictures at the beautiful lawn in front of the walls of the old shrine, even standing in front of double doors that looked as old as Texas itself before they walked through those doors and into the past, to places like what was known as the Long Barrack, where so many of the brave men who lost their lives against the Mexican Army made their last stand.

And there was another one of Clay's favorites, the Wall of History, what had been the north wall when the great Colonel William Travis had made his own last stand.

Clay loved it all, loved that wall and the Cavalry Courtyard and the Alamo Garden and all the flags, including the one of Texas. The year he'd turned ten, his parents had even rented out Alamo Hall for a birthday party, his favorite of all time.

Remember the Alamo?

No way Clay Hollis would ever forget what happened here.

He'd stand in front of the huge sign that said THE BIRTH OF THE REPUBLIC OF TEXAS and read every word all over again, even though he was pretty sure that if he had to, he could recite most of it from memory. This was history that never felt like work to him, that really was burned into his memory and his heart and what his mom liked to call his old Texas soul.

Clay had this way of moving around so that he was hardly ever with other people, like these were different kinds of moves than the ones he used on a football field. If he kept moving and picked his spots, he was able to keep finding the thing he liked best at the Alamo: the quiet. Maybe yesterday's game against the Vikings had followed him all the way home last night because Coach had come for dinner. But it hadn't followed him here, to where the ghosts of old San Antonio were.

Somehow, in Clay's mind, it made the men who had fought and died here even braver because—in the end, anyway—they knew they didn't have a chance against General Santa Anna and his firepower and his army. The sad part was that they all died not knowing that in a big way they'd really won, that their fight here was the real beginning of Texas's independence.

They died not knowing they'd be legends.

They were surrounded and outnumbered, but wouldn't quit. They knew they had no chance without reinforcements, reinforcements that wouldn't get to them in time. But even when the cannonballs began to destroy the Alamo's walls, they kept fighting, even going from room to room and engaging in hand-to-hand combat until the very end.

It was just one more reason why "Remember the Alamo!" became a rallying cry for the rest of the Texas army, why people thought the spirit of Colonel Travis and Davy Crockett and the rest of them was what helped General Sam Houston force Santa Anna's men back across the Rio Grande after the Battle of San Jacinto, why Sam Houston was remembered as a great hero of Texas as well.

He just wasn't remembered the way the men of the Alamo were.

Clay wandered around outside now, feeling the sun on him as the day began to warm, finally making his way to his favorite plaque of all, the one with William Travis's letter written on it.

It was addressed "To the People of Texas and all Americans in the world—Fellow citizens & compatriots." Clay always looked at it and thought it was the cool olden-days version of Instagram, or a Facebook post.

But this was a letter Colonel Travis wrote a couple of weeks before he died at the north wall:

> *I am besieged, by a thousand or more*
> *of the Mexicans under Santa Anna—I*
> *have sustained a continual Bombardment*
> *& cannonade for 24 hours & have not*
> *lost a man—The enemy has demanded*
> *a surrender at discretion, otherwise the*
> *garrison are to be put to the sword, if the fort*
> *is taken—I have answered the demand with*
> *a cannon shot, & our flag still waves proudly*
> *from the walls.*

Clay loved the part about the flag. It was as if Colonel Travis wanted everybody to see what he could see from inside those walls, which he already knew were coming down.

The best part of the letter, though, came near the end.

> *I shall never surrender or retreat. Then, I*
> *call on you in the name of Liberty, of patriotism*
> *& everything dear to the American character to*
> *come to our aid, with all dispatch—The enemy*
> *is receiving reinforcements daily and will no*
> *doubt increase to three or four thousand in four*
> *or five days.*
>
> *If this call is neglected, I am determined to*
> *sustain myself for as long as possible & die like a*
> *soldier who never forgets what is due to his own*
> *honor & that of his country—Victory or Death*
>
> *William Barret Travis*
> *Lt. Col. Comdt*

Every time Clay read it, every single time, this place really did feel like a shrine to him, like church, and not just on Sundays.

"Pretty awesome," a girl's voice said, and he turned to see Maddie Guerrero, even though he hadn't seen or heard her coming up behind him, because he was that fixed on Colonel Travis's letter.

"You shouldn't sneak up on people that way," he said.

"I didn't sneak up on anybody," Maddie said.

"Could have said hello."

"Hello," she said, giving him a big smile.

Clay couldn't help himself. He smiled back at her. Maddie usually made him smile, at least when he hadn't just messed up in a game or was walking off a big hit. She was a year younger than he was and she was his best friend's kid sister, but Clay still liked being around her.

A lot.

He wasn't sure if that meant he *liked* her. He wasn't willing to go that far. But he knew that he just felt better about things when he was with her at school or at practice or at a game or when he was just hanging around at the Guerrero house. He knew how glad he was when he found out she was going to be team manager for the Stars.

But they were hardly ever alone. There were always other people around. Other kids at school. Guys on the team. David. Or David and Bryce Darrell, when they'd all be together at David's house.

Suddenly, though, it was just the two of them, standing in front of Colonel Travis's letter.

"If I startled you so much, I could leave," she said, still smiling.

"No!" Clay said, immediately thinking that came out a lot hotter than he'd intended.

"Don't worry," she said. "I'm not going anywhere."

Sometimes he couldn't believe she was younger than he was. There was something about her, Clay thought, that just seemed older.

"Are you by yourself?" he said.

She nodded. "I like coming here by myself."

"Same," Clay said. He tilted his head at her. "Your parents let you?"

"You mean, come by myself?" Maddie said. "Does that surprise you?" She narrowed her eyes, but Clay knew she wasn't really mad. "Because I'm a girl, or because I'm eleven?"

He laughed. "Are you sure you're only eleven?"

She laughed, too. A good, loud, happy sound. But then Maddie Guerrero was one of the happiest people Clay knew.

"You never told me you liked coming to the Alamo," he said.

"You never asked me," she said. "But anybody who doesn't like coming here is a complete idiot."

"Agreed."

"Mom and Dad aren't coming home from their trip until later this afternoon," she said. "David and our babysitter are having breakfast a couple of blocks up, that place David says has the best huevos rancheros in San Antonio. I told them if I wanted eggs that way, I could make them at home. And that I'd rather come here."

She pointed at the plaque, the P.S. from Colonel Travis after he signed his name, where he started out saying that the Lord was on the side of him and his men.

Maddie said, "He says that when the enemy showed up, they couldn't even find three bushels of corn. I figure if they could go without eating, so can I."

Clay said, "This letter is the best thing here."

"My dad says that a lot of people talk about duty and honor and country and all stuff like that," Maddie said. "But these guys lived it."

"And died it."

"Totally!" Maddie said. Then she said, "You want to wander a little bit?"

"Totally," Clay said.

So they walked around, taking their time, sometimes standing with other people, sometimes not. Maddie liked the front room of the shrine, standing under a huge chandelier. She asked if he wanted to go see the room that used to be a burial chamber for the monks, and Clay said he would, but it always felt to him like he was passing through a cemetery.

"Are you kidding?" she said. "This whole place is like a cemetery!"

He told her he had to admit she made a good point.

"You think it's something you can learn," he said to her, "being as brave as these guys were?"

"It's in all of us," she said. "We just don't know how much of it we have until we need it."

They went all the way to the back of the shrine, where flags were mounted on the walls, the two highest being the American flag and the Lone Star flag of Texas.

"Nothing against the Stars and Stripes," Clay said, "but I like ours better."

"The way I look at it," Maddie said, "is that you've got one really solid star, why do you need a bunch of others?"

Before long they were moving slowly along the Wall of History. Maddie was the one doing most of the talking now, maybe showing off a little, like she wanted to impress Clay with her own knowledge of this place and its history, sounding a little bit like an eleven-year-old tour guide.

"You know how Colonel Travis's letter got out, right?" she said.

Clay decided to impress her right back.

"He gave it to a courier," he said. "A man named Martin."

Now Maddie came back at him, as if this were a one-on-one game of Alamo trivia. "*Albert* Martin."

"I knew that."

She shrugged, and grinned. "Well, you say you do."

"Don't mess with me on Alamo stuff, girl," he said. "I've *forgotten* more than most people remember."

"Sorrr-ry," she said.

"Do you know what was written on the envelope that had the letter inside it?"

She put her hands on her hips. "Are you really asking me that?" she said. "'Victory or death!'"

It came out loudly enough for people down the wall to turn and stare at her. At both of them. Clay didn't care, the way he didn't care about the one o'clock football games right now. He just didn't want this morning to end. He kept waiting for Maddie's phone to either make some kind of noise or vibrate, have her check it and tell him that her babysitter was coming to pick her up. But it hadn't happened yet.

This had turned into one of the best visits Clay had ever made to the Alamo, even better than his birthday party here, until they were seated on a bench in the Cavalry Courtyard.

That was when Maddie brought up the Vikings game.

"I was having such a nice day," Clay said. "Why do we have to talk about *yester*day?"

"I know you want to," she said.

"I want to talk about how I cost us that game?" Clay said. "No, I don't."

"You only *think* you don't want to talk about it," Maddie said. "You being a boy and all, and boys not wanting to talk about their feelings."

"Here's what I'm feeling," he said. "That I *don't* want to talk about the game."

She giggled. "But, see," she said, "you already *are* talking about it."

"Going back over the game isn't going to change anything."

"It's not the whole game, silly. It's just one play. How long can that take?"

He leaned back and closed his eyes. Here he was, surrounded by all the history about the bravest group of men Texas had ever known. But Maddie Guerrero, whose brother had thrown the pass yesterday, wanted to talk about a ball he could have caught and should have caught except that he'd chickened out.

"Too long," he said.

She turned and faced him, pulling her knees up in front of her.

"Listen," she said, "we all saw what you did."

"More like what I *didn't*," Clay said.

"Okay, what you didn't. And nobody could believe it, starting with me, because you always make that catch, no matter how many guys are around you."

"Thanks for reminding me," he said. "I'm feeling much better already."

"I mean, I know you pulled up on that one ball last week, too.

But I just figured that could happen to anybody, even somebody like you, as good as you are."

She talked fast. Even sitting next to her on this bench, Clay felt as if he were running hard to keep up with her.

"You think I'm good?" he said.

"Don't be an idiot," she said. "Or treat me like one about football. I know you already know how much *I* know about football. So you don't need me to tell you what an awesome receiver you are."

Maybe sometimes I do, Clay thought.

"Did your brother tell you to talk to me?" he said.

"Okay, now you are being an idiot," she said. "Did you tell him you were coming here today?"

Clay shook his head.

"He didn't know you were going to be here, so how could he have known I'd run into you?" Maddie said. "I didn't even know I was going to bring up that play till I did, if you want to know the truth. Actually, that happens with me a lot, sometimes it's like my brain is trying to keep up with my mouth."

"Hadn't picked up on that."

"Is that supposed to be funny, Mr. Funny Man?"

"Guess not."

"Back to the game."

"Or not."

"Here's the thing," she said, "not that you officially asked me for my opinion. You can't let this turn into a thing." She stared at him, eyes wide. "And don't dare tell me I don't know what I'm talking about because I'm a girl."

"Wasn't going to," Clay said. "I know you know your stuff. And your brother tells me all the time how much football you know."

That got her attention. "Really?" she said. "He said that?"

Clay said, "Hey, if I didn't need you to tell me I'm a good player, you don't need me or David to tell you that you know as much football as any boy we know."

"Well," she said, "you got me there."

"Let me ask you something," he said. "What did your brother say about the interception?"

"Nothing," she said. "He doesn't talk much about the game when it's over."

"But now you are."

"Hey," she said. "I know all I am is the manager. But I still feel like I'm part of the team, and not just because my brother's the QB. And I know that if you do let this turn into a thing, it's not only going to mess you up, it's going to mess the team up. And don't get mad at me for saying that."

"Get mad at Maddie, you mean?"

"Gee, never heard that one before," she said. Then: "So what do you think?"

"I think you're right," he said.

"That it's a thing, or that you can't let it become one?"

"Both," he said. "And please don't tell David I said that."

"If we're going to be friends," Maddie said, "you're gonna have to know that you can trust me."

Friends. Him and Maddie. He would have signed up for that when his day began.

"Okay," he said. "But I felt like more than just another chump-wit yesterday. I felt like a coward."

"Oh, stop it!" she said. "So you weren't as tough as you wanted to be on one catch. It doesn't make you *that*."

"You sure?"

"Sure, I'm sure."

"How come you seem to know so much stuff, period?"

She sighed, and smiled again. "*Not* sure about that," she said. "But I seem to come by it naturally."

"Weren't you a little afraid about bringing this up?"

Maddie said, "Me? Now I'm *really* not afraid of anything, except maybe spiders."

Somehow, he felt better, if not any tougher. He knew you couldn't make yourself get tougher just because you came to visit Colonel Travis and his men. He knew he wasn't going to know if that play yesterday really had turned into a thing until the Stars played their next game, next Saturday. And a loss was a loss was a loss, whether you talked it out or not.

But he'd gained a friend today, and that was why—for the first time all weekend—Clay felt like he'd won something, like the weekend wasn't a *total* loss after all.

# EIGHT

**T**HEY HAD A GOOD PRACTICE on Thursday night, their last before Saturday's game against the Bears.

But then Clay had never thought there was any such thing as a bad practice. It was the way he thought about football games on television: There was no such thing as a bad one; some were just better than others. The way Clay looked at it, you were still competing at practice, even if it was against your own teammates and sometimes yourself. You were in pads, you were doing some hitting, and you were getting hit. It was football. No such thing as a bad day.

Clay had managed to put together two stellar practices in a row. Mostly he'd done this by trying to keep things as simple as possible. He was worrying about just two things: route; ball. Worry about the process, not the result. It had all started with a tip from his dad, not about football, but golf.

Ben Hollis never talked to Clay about technique. He said he knew as much about being a wide receiver as he did about being an astronaut, so his biggest contribution to Clay's pass-catching ability was staying the heck out of his way and letting him play the

56

game. But every once in a while, he would give Clay a tip about his mental game, because, he said, the principles about getting your mind right traveled real well from sport to sport.

They had talked a little bit about what happened in the Vikings game, once a couple of days had passed, Clay's dad telling him that there wasn't an athlete alive who didn't suffer a case of the nerves from time to time. And he said the place where nerves showed up the most in golf was with putting, sometimes with putts so short you felt as if you could kick them in with your foot.

"Not with you," Clay said.

His dad made a snorting sound. "Happens all the time!" he said. "And what I do when I feel my hands shaking as I stand over a three-footer, and my brain is spinning around with all kinds of bad thoughts about what will happen if I miss, I make myself go back to fundamentals: Hit it exactly this far, with six inches of break. Or a foot of break. Whatever it is. Pick out a piece of grass or dirt and just think about that instead of the hole. Before long I'm back to thinking putting's as easy as it was when I was your age, and I had no fear."

"So you weren't afraid in golf," Clay said. "What about football?"

His dad had put an arm around him and said, "Came and went."

"What about Coach saying you can't play if you're afraid?"

His dad grinned and said, "Maybe he forgot when he was."

For two practices, Clay had been telling himself to run down the field five yards, or ten, make his cut. If he was the intended receiver, see the ball and catch it. Then repeat.

It was working for him. He wouldn't know how well it was working until it was all for real on Saturday and the guys guarding him were on their side and not his. What his dad told him had sunk in, though, at least for now. Clay was just trying to control the things he could control. And he'd made it through Tuesday's practice and tonight's practice without a single drop.

They were about to end Thursday's practice the way they ended a lot of them for Coach Monty Cooper: offense with the ball on the defense's twenty-yard line. Sometimes the offense got four downs to try to get themselves a score, sometimes they got two.

Tonight? One.

Coach Coop loved this drill, because they knew they had to throw and so did the defense. Sometimes he let David Guerrero make the call, but tonight Coach came into the huddle and told them he had the play that was going to send them home happy and force them boys on the defense to run two laps.

"Listen up, Danny," he said.

Clay felt himself smiling and could see David doing the same behind his face mask. Every player on the Stars was used to Coach calling him the wrong name by now, most of them more than once, often by different names. It had reached the point that when he called Clay "Colt," Clay's head would whip around anyway, out of force of habit. Coach liked to joke on himself and say he'd even been better at marriage than he was at remembering people's names.

Sometimes he'd just give up and call them all by the same name: "Hoss."

In this moment, though, David was Danny.

"Yeah, Coach," he said.

"This is what it would be like at the end of a half or end of a game, when we're down to our last shot," Coach said. "And you know what that means, right, Danny Boy?"

"We got to put it in the end zone?"

"There you go," Coach said. "This is when it's all pure ball, when you're looking those other boys in the eyes and saying that you know your best is better'n theirs."

Clay was watching him. He looked completely happy, or at least as happy as he could ever be now that he didn't get to put on a uniform anymore.

"Pure one-hundred-percent American-made football," Coach Coop said. He turned and spit and then started walking away from the huddle. "Now run that thing just like I drew it up."

It wasn't the first time this had happened, either, Coach getting to talking, getting excited about what was about to happen, and forgetting that he hadn't told them what pure-ball play he wanted them to run.

"Coach," Clay said, "you better give us the call, before you have to call a delay of game penalty on yourself."

Coach turned around with a look on his face he'd get sometimes, like he was still in uniform, and had been caught doing something wrong. "Hoss," he said to Clay, "thanks for reminding me," and gave a soft slap to the side of Clay's helmet. Then he leaned back in, over David's shoulder, and said, "Deep cross." And spit again, like he was punctuating the sentence.

It was one of Clay's favorite plays, maybe because it was so basic. He lined up wide right, Will Kellerman lined up wide left. They each ran fifteen yards, like they were running straight go patterns, then cut toward the middle of the field, and toward each other.

Coach said that in a perfect world, they'd come so close to each other that the boys on defense guarding them would bump into each other like bowling pins.

"Try to make sure you're the one open," David said to Clay.

"Whatever you say, Danny!" Clay said to him.

Route, ball. Only things that mattered right now. Practice like you play.

David was in the shotgun. Jalen King, their best cover guy, was guarding Clay. Kyle Murphy was on Will. Their two safeties had already dropped back to the five-yard line before the ball was snapped. They didn't care if somebody caught the ball in front of them. They just didn't want anybody getting behind them on the last play of practice, because they didn't want to be the ones who had to run laps in what was still ninety-plus-degree heat, even at seven o'clock.

Clay and Will timed their cuts perfectly. Not only that, if somebody had been taking video of the play, they would have seen that they passed each other almost at the exact center of the field at East San Antonio Middle School, right in line with the goalposts.

Jalen King got slowed up enough in all the traffic that Clay broke free from him, was running free now toward the pylon at the goal line. Out of the corner of his eye, though, he saw a very large object coming from his left, and at a very high speed, a large object that could only be Bryce Darrell. Who *always* practiced like he played, even if that meant putting one of his best buds on the ground, with absolutely no mercy.

Clay had run his route. That part of the mission had been accomplished.

Now all he had to worry about was the ball he saw coming his way, the same as Bryce was.

*Not tonight,* Clay told himself.

*No nerves tonight.*

Clay looked the ball into his hands, pulled it in, angled his body to the right, toward the left pylon just as Bryce sent him flying, Clay landing a yard into the end zone, ball still firmly in his arms.

Pure ball.

It would have been a perfect way to end his night, except that it wasn't the end of his night. That came a few minutes later. His mom was always on time and sometimes liked to watch the last few minutes of practice. But tonight she'd texted him to say that she was going to be about ten minutes late. Clay didn't care. He'd caught the ball, he'd taken Bryce's hit, he was good to go, whenever it was time to go home.

When he saw her car pulling into the lot, he turned around to take one more look at the field. The only person still there was Coach Coop, sitting alone on the bench closest to Clay, rubbing his right knee, staring straight ahead, almost like he was in some kind of trance.

Clay stared at Coach the way Coach was staring at the field, wondering if he was taking another look back at the old days.

Or if he just had no place to be.

# NINE

**S**ATURDAY'S GAME WAS AT BOB Hood Stadium at
South Lakes High School, which was on the far south side
of San Antonio. Clay's dad liked the stadium so much he
had taken Clay to a couple of Friday night games at South Lakes
last season, just to give Clay a feel—and sound—of what Friday
Night Lights were really like in Texas. The experience turned out
to be everything Ben Hollis said it would be. On the way home
that first Friday night, Clay said to his dad, "I'm ready to sign up for
high school football right now."

"Slow down, cowboy," his dad had said. "You're growing up
fast enough already for your mother and me."

Not everybody on the Stars had seen the stadium, though. When
they'd taken their end of the field for stretching David Guerrero
took a good look around and said to Clay, "What year are they
going to play the Super Bowl here?"

Bryce Darrell said, "Shoot, these fields all look the same to me
once I started tackling people."

Clay was standing between Bryce and David. "Ask you a
question, BD?" he said.

"Long as it's not a hard one," Bryce said. "I'm starting to get my game thing on."

Clay grinned at him. "If I told you that you'd never have to go to school again, but the one condition was that you could never play football again, would you sign on for that deal?"

Clay couldn't decide whether Bryce looked shocked at the question, or just plain insulted.

"I can't believe that you even had to ask me that," Bryce said.

"So, even if you never had to go to English or math or history again, you still wouldn't give up hitting people?"

*"Hail no,"* he said, which was his Texas way of pronouncing hell. He looked at Clay then and said, "You ready?"

"You know I am," Clay said.

Even with the day he'd had with Maddie at the Alamo and the two good practices during the week, this still felt like one of the longest weeks of Clay's life. Yeah. He was ready. Just not in the same way Bryce was. He couldn't wait to get out there so he *could* start hitting people. Clay was more anxious about somebody hitting him.

"How we looking?" Maddie said to Clay behind the bench, maybe five minutes before the kick.

Clay put out his fist so she could bump it. "Victory or death," he said.

"Okaaaaaay," she said. "At least we're not being too dramatic."

"Kidding," he said. "I'm good."

"Good," she said. "Remember: Not a thing."

Clay said, "I have no idea what you're talking about."

*"Real* good," she said.

All week long the only thing Clay had really been afraid of was that this Saturday would never arrive.

But it had.

They all knew that the Bears' best player was still their middle linebacker, Ty Nobles. He'd been their best player when he was ten and eleven and now at twelve. And seemed to have gotten a lot bigger in the last year.

"Guy's a total freak," Bryce said. "And coming from me, you know that's a compliment."

Players on both teams were lining up for the opening kickoff. Bryce was agitated that the Bears had won the toss and elected to defer, meaning they wanted to start the game on defense and then get the ball to start the second half. It meant that Bryce would have to wait to get his own freak on and put somebody on the ground.

"The only sad thing about both me and Ty being middle linebackers," Bryce said, "is that we don't get to find out with each other who can hit harder."

"Tragic," David Guerrero said.

"Practically a crime," Clay said.

"You know sometimes I worry that you two don't get me at all," Bryce said.

As nervous as he was with the game about to start, as nervous as they all were, Clay laughed.

"Dude," he said, "that's not the problem. The problem is that we get you *too* well."

"It's why we never do anything to make you even more ornery than you already are," David said.

"How's about we just play ornery today?" Bryce said, shifting his weight back and forth, quickly, from one foot to another, the way he did when he wasn't in the game.

Clay thought: I just don't want to walk away from this game ornery about *me*.

His first test came early, the way he'd hoped it would. Third offensive play of the game. Coach sent in a slant pass, David to Clay. All David was supposed to do was take the snap, straighten up, make his throw to Clay as soon as Clay made his cut.

Clay knew that he'd be running right into Ty Nobles's area. He told himself it was a good thing. Maybe he could find out what he needed to find out right now.

*Let's do this.*

He didn't know the kid covering him; he must have been new to the Bears this season. But whoever he was, he was giving Clay way more room than he needed to, as if he wasn't paying close enough attention to down and distance. Or maybe he'd heard how fast Clay was from some of his teammates and didn't want Clay to burn him deep even though the game had just started.

Clay was so anxious to get to where he needed to be, to get the ball, that he nearly jumped David's snap count. But didn't. Came from the right. Hadn't even run five yards toward the middle when David put a hard—like everything-he-had hard—ball on Clay's numbers. The ball caught him under his pads and nearly took the breath out of him. Didn't. Sometimes the bullet passes were the easiest for him to hold on to, and Clay did that now, knowing he had control, knowing he had the first down. Then he got popped right away by Ty, his shoulder pad putting a direct hit on the ball. Clay held on as he went down, cradling the ball with both arms, making sure it wouldn't come loose when he hit the ground. When he *did* hit the ground, he landed on the ball, which did take the air out of him.

Clay didn't care.

He popped right up. They always talked about getting back up in sports after you got knocked down. Clay did that now, fast as he could manage. Maybe he was getting back up in more ways than one. Still a long way to go today. But already this Saturday was better than the last one. And different, maybe.

"Good catch," Ty said.

Clay nodded. "Good hit," he said.

The Stars took it down the field from there, mixing runs to Josh Bodeen with throws to Clay and Will on the outside. On first and goal from the nine-yard line David faked a handoff to Josh, waited for Clay to clear the corner, and lofted a perfect lob pass to Clay in the corner of the end zone. Again he looked the ball right into his hands, didn't stop looking at it until it was in his hands and he had to make sure he was inbounds. He was. It was 6–0, Stars. David made an even better fake to Josh on the conversion, sold it was well as a Pop Warner quarterback could, kept the ball himself for a bootleg on the left side, where Clay had lined up. Clay laid a perfect block on Ty Nobles, even managed to put him on his backside. Then he helped him up when the play was over.

"Hey?" Ty said. "Looks like I'm gonna have to keep a closer eye on you."

"I'm already keeping both eyes on *you*," Clay said. He gave Ty a light slap on the side of his helmet. Ty did the same to him. They were letting each other know that they knew exactly what was going on here:

Pure ball.

The Bears scored on their first possession, too, but Bryce came on a blitz and batted down their pass for the conversion. It was 7–6, Stars. Right before the half, Coach Coop called for the same crossing pattern they'd used at the end of practice the other night. It was Will who broke clear this time, managed to get to the sideline as the kid covering him slipped, then ran fifty more yards for the score.

Stars at the half, 13–6.

The third quarter was scoreless, but midway through the fourth quarter, the Stars were driving again. Clay caught another ball over the middle, got hit by both Ty and the cornerback after he did, almost at the same time. But he held on. In traffic. Again. He was back to being that guy. The guy who could make that kind of catch. At least for today.

They all knew the way Bryce and the guys on defense had been getting after it since they'd allowed the Bears their one score. So another score for the Stars here, they were all pretty sure, would mean game over.

"Let's put 'er in the books," was the way Coach had put it at the start of the drive.

They had a first down just inside the Bears' thirty-yard line when Coach decided to go for it all. It was right after the Bears had called their first timeout of the second half. David had gone over to the sideline to talk to Coach Coop and brought the play back with him.

"Hitch and go," he said when he knelt in the huddle.

He looked at Clay when he said it. The ball was coming to him. It was a simple go pattern. You came off the ball hard, slowed down about ten yards up the field like you were getting ready to make a break to your left or right.

Then you really did just *go*.

"Coach thinks old Ty might be coming on the blitz," David said. "So be looking for the ball, maybe sooner than we usually like."

"Got it," Clay said.

"Be there, is what I'm saying."

Clay grinned at him. "*You* be there."

Then they nodded at each other. The ball would be there. So would Clay. That was their deal, the way things had always worked for them, at least most of the time.

The cornerback bit when Clay slowed down, as he was sure he would. He wasn't giving Clay too much room this time. He wasn't giving him enough.

And was about to get burned deep.

Clay not only slowed up, he half turned and looked back, as if the ball was already on its way. The corner pinched up on him when he did. As soon as he did, Clay blew past him, down the sideline, running fast and free.

Now he turned for the ball for real, maybe a beat before he heard somebody in the defensive backfield yell, "*Ball!*"

The pass was a little underthrown, and Clay had to come back for it. But he'd created enough space between himself and the corner covering him and the safety scrambling to get over and help out, that he had enough time to do that, even if he did have to break stride.

When you were this open you had to concentrate as hard as ever, as hard as you did in traffic, because sometimes having all the time in the world made your mind wander enough to make you miss.

Wasn't happening.

As soon as the ball was in Clay's hands, he was turning back toward the end zone and turning it on again. But he was at the ten-yard line by now, and nobody was catching him. He went into the end zone untouched, with the touchdown that made it 19–7 for the Stars.

Now he felt air coming out of him, but in a good way, in the best way. Like he could finally exhale. He had waited all week for this game to be played and couldn't have known it would be this sweet, that it would end this way, even though there was still some football left to be played.

He was so lost in the excitement of the moment, the thrill of the moment, that it wasn't until he handed the ball to the ref and turned back toward the field that he processed that none of his teammates had come running down the field to pound on him, to celebrate the moment with him.

It was because so many of them were standing in the Stars' backfield, or moving in that direction. It turned out that Ty Nobles *had* come on a blitz, just as Coach Coop had predicted. He'd gotten through everybody and gone crashing into David Guerrero an instant before David released the ball. *That* was why Clay had to come back for the ball a little bit. That was why the ball had been underthrown.

Now Clay could see that David was down.

And not getting up.

Now Clay was running, back toward his quarterback and best friend, not away from him.

# TEN

**B**Y THE TIME CLAY GOT to David, he was at least sitting up.

Will Kellerman's dad, a doctor, was kneeling next to him. Coach was walking back to the Stars' bench, where David's parents were waiting for him. They were football parents. Maybe they'd been on their way onto the field when David was still down. But now he was up, even if he was only halfway up. They were staying where they were, for now. Clay was pretty sure his mom and dad would handle things the same way it if were him.

Maddie was right there, though, standing with the other players, her eyes big. Clay didn't know her well enough, not yet, to know what really scared her. But she looked scared enough right now. After telling Clay the other day not to be scared by football, now football had done it to her.

Clay stood next to her, both of them close enough to Dr. Kellerman to hear what he was saying.

"David," he said, "have you been conscious the whole time since your head hit the ground?"

David's helmet was off. He turned to look at Dr. Kellerman,

but seemed to be moving in slow motion. "You mean have I been awake?"

"Yes."

"Yes," David said.

"You didn't even go away for even a few seconds?"

"No."

"For sure?"

"For sure."

"Do you feel sick to your stomach?" Dr. Kellerman said. "Like you even might want to throw up?"

"No, sir. It's not my stomach feeling dizzy, just my head a little bit."

It was then that David looked past Will's dad and saw Clay standing with Maddie. Bryce was on the other side of Maddie.

"Clay?" David said.

"Right here, man."

"Did we score?"

For the first time Clay started to feel better. As hard as David must have hit his head—Clay still didn't know exactly what had happened—that head of his was still in the game.

"We scored," Clay said. "Perfect throw. Even I couldn't drop it."

For the first time Clay looked down and noticed that Maddie was holding her brother's helmet by the face mask in her right hand.

David managed a small smile.

"Cool," he said.

"The only thing annoying me," Clay said, "is that now you've settled the argument on which one of us is better at taking a hit."

"Sure about that?" David Guerrero said.

"I hate to interrupt the conversation," Dr. Kellerman said, "but could everybody back up just a bit and give us a little more room? Pretend I've got David in my office." He grinned. "Alone." Then he called over to the ref closest to him and said he was going to need just a couple of more minutes.

Clay and his teammates backed off about five yards. Maddie did the same. When they were out of David's earshot, Clay whispered to Maddie, "What happened?"

"Ty blew past everybody," she said, her own voice barely above a whisper. "My brother didn't see him until the last possible moment. If he had, maybe he could have covered up and protected the stupid ball and taken a hit. But it was too late. And that's not him, anyway. I don't even know how he got as much on the ball as he did."

"That *is* him," Clay said.

"He had no chance to break his fall once Ty went into him," she said. "At the last second Ty even tried to wrap him up with both arms, so's they could hit the ground together. Too late for that, too. My brother was going straight backward. Then the only thing that did break his fall was the back of his helmet."

Clay thought the football girl might cry then. He didn't want that to happen, knew she probably didn't want it to happen, but didn't know how he could stop it from happening.

But she got saved, maybe they both did, because it was at that moment that Dr. Kellerman started to help David to his feet. As soon as he did, Clay was past his teammates in a blink, even Bryce, who was closer to David. Dr. Kellerman was on David's left side.

Clay got on his right and carefully placed David's throwing arm around his shoulder.

Sometimes you got back up yourself, and sometimes you needed help.

"I got you," Clay said.

They heard the sound of applause from the people in the stands. To Clay it was the sound of the same relief he was feeling.

"Steady as we go," Dr. Kellerman said.

The fans kept applauding as they began to move toward the sideline. So did players from both teams.

"You okay?" Clay said.

"Compared to what?" David said.

Clay felt as if they were taking baby steps as he and Dr. Kellerman walked David along. When they finally got to the Stars' bench, Dr. Kellerman said to David's mom and dad, "He took a pretty good knock. But, all in all, he's fine."

Clay could see David's mom, Elena, trying to act calm.

"I will never complain about you having a hard head ever again," she said. She put a hand on his shoulder. "How are you feeling?"

"My head feels about the same as it does when I'm studying," David said.

"Okay," Elena Guerrero said, "now I *am* concerned."

"Hey," David said. "Hey, all you guys. I'm fine."

Dr. Kellerman said to David's dad, "Alejandro, why don't you go ahead and pull your car around behind the stands over there?"

"Where's he going?" Clay said to Dr. Kellerman. "You said he was okay."

"Just over to the hospital," he said, quickly adding, "Strictly routine when somebody does get a knock to the head like David did. Promise."

"I'm going, too," Maddie said.

"What a good manager and a good sister does," Dr. Kellerman said, smiling at her. "Takes care of the players."

From behind them Clay heard a whistle blow. The ref who'd blown it was waving players from both teams back into position for the Stars' conversion attempt, almost like he was reminding them that there was still a game going on here.

It was then that Josh Bodeen, who was their best backup quarterback, went over to Coach Coop and asked if he should go in for David now.

Coach didn't seem to hear Josh at first. His back was to the field, and he was watching Dr. Kellerman help David into the backseat of Mr. Guerrero's black SUV, right before he closed the door and the car slowly moved away. Clay just figured Doc was driving himself to the hospital.

"Coach?" Josh said again. "You want I should go in for David?"

Coach seemed to snap out of it then, and turned back toward the field.

"Sure," he said. "You got a play?"

"No, sir."

Clay stepped up. "How about we run that rollout where Josh can either keep it or throw it to me?"

"Sounds good," Coach said, then turned around one last time, but the SUV was long gone.

Then he looked at Clay and said, "I sure hope that boy is okay."

Monty Cooper squeezed his eyes shut, kept them shut, then opened them. And for this one moment, there and gone, Clay though it might be his tough old coach fighting back tears.

They won the game but lost David.

He called Clay as soon as he was home from the hospital and told him it was a concussion.

"Bad one?" Clay said, not sure if there was any such thing as a good one.

"Doc Kellerman says it's a mild one," David said, "even though he says there's no such thing as mild when it happens to somebody our age. But my mom was way ahead of him. She said, 'You know what a minor concussion is? One that happens to somebody else's kid.'"

"I hear you," Clay said. "*My* mom was watching one of the pregame shows, I can't remember which one, and one of the guys was talking about minor surgery and she said pretty much the same thing. Minor surgery is somebody else's."

Neither one of them said anything until Clay finally said, "I know this sounds like a stupid question. But does your head hurt?"

"What hurts," David said, "is that I don't know when I can play again."

"But Doc said it was mild."

"It is," David said. "Except that in football now, it's like *concussion* is the dirtiest word in the English language."

"But you're not, like, out for the season or anything, right?"

Clay knew the only thing worse than him missing the rest of

the season would be if David missed it. They weren't just on a team together. They *were* a team.

"Oh, I'm gonna power through, don't worry about me," David said. "But under the new rules, I have to sit out at least one game."

"Then you're good to go?"

"Maybe."

"What does maybe mean?"

"Let me read you something," David said, "from the league's concussion policy."

Clay waited.

David said, "You still there?"

Clay was about to make a joke and say, no, he was actually off fixing himself a sandwich. But this was serious stuff. When something happened to one of them, good or bad, it happened to both of them. They were as close as brothers, and maybe closer, because most brothers Clay knew fought sometimes and he and David never did. The closest Clay could remember to them fighting about something was when David had called him out for pulling up on that pass route.

"Okay," David said, "here goes: 'Any Pop Warner participant who has been removed from practice, play, or competition due to a head injury or suspected concussion may not return to Pop Warner activities until the participant has been evaluated by a correctly licensed medical professional trained in the evaluation and management of concussions and receives written clearance to return to play from that licensed practitioner.'"

"Please tell me that's all there is," Clay said.

"There's more—my mom printed the whole thing out for

me—but that's the big stuff. Before I can play again, I can't just get cleared by Doc Kellerman, I have to be cleared by some kind of brain doctor."

"Like Will Smith in the movie."

"My mom is so stuck on this you can't believe it."

"Oh," Clay said. "I can believe it."

"Forgot your mom thinks *she's* the brain doctor."

There was another silence, like they were both caught in what they didn't know, until Clay said, "It'll be just one game, wait and see."

"Now look at who's the brain doctor," David Guerrero said.

"You want me to come over?"

David lowered his voice. "My mom says I've got to take it easy the rest of the day." Now his voice was so low Clay could barely hear him. "And my sister's being worse than my mom."

In the background, Clay heard Maddie say, "I heard that!"

"Sounds like you'd rather mess with Ty Nobles than with her," Clay said.

"Tell me about it."

"Tell you about *what*?" Clay heard Maddie say now. "What did he say?"

"How great he thinks you are."

Both Clay and Maddie said, "Shut up," at almost the same time.

Clay told him to feel better, and that he'd check on him tomorrow, then ended the call. There was a Longhorns game starting in about half an hour. They were on the road today against Baylor, and he knew his dad was going to want to watch it with him. And Clay knew he would, even though this might be the only day of the whole season when he wasn't interested in watching guys bang on one another. He wasn't footballed out, exactly. He'd never be totally footballed out. But right now he still couldn't shake the image of David lying flat on his back.

Or thinking all over again about what his mom really called concussions:

Brain wounds.

Now David had one. And was going to miss one game, at least, because of it. Even when you were twelve—or especially when you were twelve—even missing one Saturday felt like you were missing a lot more. Like it was a whole month of Saturdays.

Where Clay really wanted to be right now was in his back-yard, running pass patterns for David. Or maybe just go back in time a few hours, and change the pass play Coach had called to a draw play. Or a quick slant. Anything that kept Ty Nobles off David.

He stayed in his room until the Texas game started and watched it with his dad until halftime. It was time for dinner, but that was all right, the Longhorns were already winning 37–7 by then.

"How did David sound when you talked to him on the phone?" Katherine Hollis said at the dinner table, over fried chicken and mashed potatoes, saying that if Clay ever needed comfort food, tonight was the night.

"Says he's probably going to have to miss a game, even though it's only a mild concussion."

Clay stepped on *mild* pretty good.

"Well, they're going to see how he's doing after a week," Clay's mom said. "That's what Elena told me."

"Mom," Clay said, "you act like his head came loose from his body or something."

"Clay Hollis," she said, "don't you take this out on me. But there's a reason why I've studied this-all the way I have, because this is what can happen. And a reason why I want to know as much as I can."

"You act like you know it all," Clay said, and was sorry as soon as the words were out of his mouth. Because he knew it sounded like he'd called her a know-it-all.

Her eyes narrowed. "Is that a smart remark, young man?"

"Now, that would be really *dumb*," Clay said.

It got a smile out of her.

"Just remember, Mom, that it happened to David, not me."

"Could've been."

"You think I don't know that?"

In a soft voice, his dad, who'd been sitting this one out even though he was sitting right there with them, said, "Clay, you know we're all on the same team: you, me, your mom, even David's mom."

"I know."

When they'd finished dinner, and after Clay had helped clear the table, he said he'd wait and have dessert later, while he and his dad were watching the LSU-Alabama game, a big one even early in the season. Then he asked his parents if it was all right if he went for a walk just to clear his head a little bit after everything that had happened today, a day when he'd had about one minute to be happy about that touchdown catch.

His mom said fine, as long as he didn't wander too far. And to make sure he took his phone with him.

"So you can track me?" Clay said.

She smiled at him again. "You said that, not me."

He was a couple of blocks from the house when he heard some-body call out his name. Clay turned and saw it was Coach Coop, behind the wheel of his truck, the window on the driver's side down.

"Hey, Coach," Clay said. "What in the heck are you doing here?"

Coach Monty Cooper squinted at Clay, the way you did when the sun was in your face.

"Beats me," he said.

# ELEVEN

**C**LAY AND HIS PARENTS LIVED on the edge of Alamo Heights. Just having that name attached to his own neighborhood gave Clay one more connection to the Alamo.

Most of the houses in the neighborhood were old, which was fine with him. The parts of San Antonio he liked the best were the old parts.

He watched Coach get out of the truck now, groaning as he did. Anytime Coach Coop had to get out of a seat or into one, it was a process.

"Knees stiffen up on me when I set awhile," he said, and not for the first time. "Course they stiffen up when I'm moving, too. Or just setting on my couch watching a game."

When they were together on the sidewalk he said, "Feel like walking a bit?"

"Been walking myself," Clay said. "We could head over to Olmos Park, that's pretty close. I like it over there."

"Sounds good to me," Coach said. "Lead the way, hoss."

Clay slowed his pace to match Coach's. If he walked at his

normal speed, it would have taken him about a minute to get a block ahead of him.

"Hey," Clay said, "you didn't lock your truck."

"If somebody's fool enough to steal it," Coach said, "then they're probably fool enough to have it."

Clay really did like Olmos Park, with its playground and picnic areas, and barbecue pits and playing field and big, tall old trees. Sometimes in the summer, when they could round up enough guys, Clay and his boys would meet here and play touch football until they were all ready to drop.

"So what *are* you doing here?" Clay said.

He knew Coach lived downtown, off Broadway. It wasn't all that far from here. But not that close, either. Clay didn't think you just accidentally ended up in Alamo Heights.

By the time they got to Olmos Park, Clay could hear Coach breathing hard.

"How about we take a seat first," he said, "then chat."

It was near seven o'clock by now, but Clay knew they weren't even close to sunset. He and Coach sat on a bench at the playground where Clay's mom used to take him when he was little. Clay saw him rub one knee, hard, and then the other, with his beat-up hands and crooked fingers. One time when Coach was over for dinner and reaching for his water glass, Clay's dad said that Monty Cooper looked as if he'd been a catcher in baseball and not a football player, and spent his career taking balls off those big hands of his.

"I'd rather deal with foul balls," Coach said that night, "than what felt like the whole National Football League steppin' on me."

Now he saw Clay watching him give his knees a good working over and said, "You think the hurt will go away when they stop beating on you. But it don't. Oh, they take playing football away from you finally. Take away the practices and the game and all the time in the locker room. Just not the hurt."

"But you're always saying it was worth it."

"It's what they all say." He squinted again, into the sun still coming through the big trees. "Sure is pretty here. Can't believe I never saw this place before."

"Sure you did," Clay said. "Remember the barbecue we had here after the team was picked?"

Coach nodded.

"Well, I sure do," he said. "I must've confused this place with Franklin Park. And what's the real big one?"

"Brackenridge."

"I think I played with a guy named Brackenridge, or Breckenridge," he said. He shrugged. "Or not."

He turned his head, a big smile on his face. "You'll find out someday when you're my age," he said. "Sometimes chasing memories is like trying to chase down the fastest man on the other team."

Wasn't the first time Clay had heard that one, either.

On the other side of the playground, a little girl kept going down one of the bigger slides, running around as soon as she got to the bottom, climbing back up the steps, going down again while her mom clapped. In the distance, where the fields were, Clay thought he heard the sound of some kind of game going on. He thought about checking his phone to see what time it was. But he didn't think he'd been away from the house long enough that he needed to check in with his folks.

And he didn't want Coach to think that he was in some kind of rush to leave.

"So what are you doing over here in what my mom calls this neck of the woods?" Clay asked again. "Were you gonna drop in on us and try to score some of Mom's pie?"

Coach turned himself on the bench so he was facing Clay now. "This is just between us boys, right? And I don't mean Cowboys."

"You can always trust me, Coach," Clay said.

Coach put out his beat-up right hand. Clay realized they were shaking on it. So he did.

"Can't go no further."

"Can't and won't," Clay said.

Coach Coop took in some air and let it out and said, "I get lost sometimes." He shook his head. "Ain't that something? Even in a world where some woman on your phone can tell you how to get where you're going."

Everybody on the Stars knew that Coach carried around an old flip-top phone, but wasn't very good at operating it, which is why he hardly ever used it. One of the team moms asked Coach one time if she should send him an email or a text with the list of families in charge of postgame snacks. Coach laughed and said, "Either one, doesn't matter. You'd be better off sending a note in a bottle."

At Olmos Park, there was just the sound of the little girl laughing from across the way. If there had been a game going on, it must have ended.

Clay said, "Anybody can get lost. It happens to me when I'm riding my bike sometimes."

"No, son," Coach said. "It's not like that. It's that sometimes I get in the truck and I'm goin' along, and then can't remember *where* I'm goin'."

He stopped and said, "Between us?"

"A hundred percent."

"Like what you always give me."

Clay sat there thinking: All I wanted to do was go for a walk.

Coach said, "I haven't told this to another living soul. But now we've run into each other like this, and here we are." He turned and spit, like he did on the field. "Not that I have all that many people to tell, anyway."

Clay had never heard him go on about anything this long, except maybe his days playing with the Cowboys.

"A couple of times," Coach said, "I even had trouble finding my way home."

"You could get an iPhone," Clay said. "I could show you how to set it up and use it. There's this thing called Waze my parents use that even tells you if there's traffic ahead of you."

"You know, hoss," he said, "sometimes I wish there was some kind of chip they could put inside my brain, to make it easy to remember."

"Everybody forgets stuff," Clay said. "You should hear my dad when he can't find his reading glasses. Or his own phone. Or his car keys."

He wondered if Coach was even listening to him. It was almost as if he were talking to himself. Trying to explain himself *to* himself in some way Clay wasn't sure he really understood.

Suddenly, in a loud voice, almost a fierce voice, Coach Coop said, *"I got to make it through this season!"* He leaned back and looked up into the sky and in a much softer voice said, "I *got* to make it back on that field."

Clay knew which field he meant: the Cowboys' stadium, AT&T, in Arlington, for the Thanksgiving game where he and his old teammates would be honored. He was talking about being with his teammates again. Clay knew how Coach felt about them. But then Clay knew how he felt about David, and the rest of the guys on the Stars.

"You'll make it, Coach," Clay said. "Why wouldn't you?"

In that soft voice Coach said, "I got to at least be able to find my way there."

"You'll be fine," Clay said. "You've got your old team, and you've got our team."

"I just want this one more season," Coach said. "And I don't want parents to start looking at me cross-eyed."

Clay said, "Wait a second, Coach: You mean they don't do that already?"

It got a laugh out of him.

"How's our boy, by the way?"

"You mean David?" Clay said. "Turns out he has a concussion."

Coach slapped Clay on his knee. "Well, course I know about the concussion," he said. "His parents called and told me. I meant, how's the boy setting here with me?"

"Good, Coach. Real good. The only thing I was afraid of today on that field was losing the game."

"That's what I'm talkin' about!" Coach said, and slapped Clay on the knee again. "And with my quarterback out, I'm gonna lean on you more than ever."

Clay said the same thing he'd said to David on the field. "I'm here."

"Concussions," Coach said, pointing to his head. "You know what we called 'em when I played?"

"Not concussions?"

Coach Coop said, "We called 'em the 'cost of doin' business.'"

Then he braced his hands on the bench and lifted himself off it, saying that he'd give Clay a lift home.

Grinning as he said, "Long as you know the way."

# TWELVE

**C**LAY HAD TWO FRIENDS OVER to his house on Sunday afternoon to watch the Cowboys game: David Guerrero and Josh Bodeen.

The Cowboys were on the road against the Redskins, so what they insisted on calling a one o'clock game on the pregame shows was actually a noon game in Texas.

Clay wanted Josh to come over so they could get the jump on working together before practice on Tuesday night, figuring they could work on some basic patterns and get a feel for what throws Josh was most comfortable making, and a feel for Clay's moves, and the different speeds he used for different pass patterns.

From the time Coach had made Josh David's official backup, Josh got his share of reps at practice. He just hadn't gotten enough. He'd mostly work on fundamentals, taking snaps from under center, handing the ball off, throwing some short balls. Josh hadn't thought David would get hurt because nobody ever got hurt in Pop Warner.

A few days before their first game, Coach had said to David, "You ever get hurt?"

David had grinned at Coach Coop. "Not even my feelings."

"Good," Coach said. "I like those quarterbacks like old Brett Favre, who went to the post every damn game until there weren't no more games."

"I think that's another five dollars for the swear pot, Coach," Clay had said that night.

"Gonna end up broke if I don't watch my damn mouth," Coach said, and they'd all laughed.

But now David *was* hurt, and it was no laughing matter. He hadn't just gotten hurt, in the worst way, with a concussion. It was like the bogeyman chasing all players these days. And ex-players, too, because Clay was thinking, harder than ever, that all the concussions Monty Cooper had suffered during his own playing days were the reason he was the way he was. That meant the concussions that he knew about and the ones he didn't.

*Cost of doing business,* Coach had said to Clay at Olmos Park.

It had been David's idea for Clay to invite Josh over, not just to watch football but play some.

"Will your mom let you?" Clay said.

"Only if I promise I won't play."

"How's that going to work?"

"Well, when I say *play,* I mean play a game," David said. "Isn't that the way it works with you?"

Clay had felt himself smiling. "Totally."

"Plus," David added, "you are totally not qualified to be a quarterback's coach, which is what I'm going to have to be for one game at least. Guys who play your position always think they know way more about mine than they do."

"Yeah," Clay said. "Go with that."

"Tell you all the time: Only guy who knows your moves better than you do is *me*."

"I know you keep saying that," Clay said. "Maybe you've been dizzy for a long time and I just didn't notice."

"Oh, that's nice," David said. "Make fun of a guy who took one for the team."

"Take your phone away from your ear and get over here," Clay said.

"On my way. Just not to play."

"That would be so wrong."

The Cowboys got up a couple of touchdowns on the Redskins right before the half and as soon as they did, Clay and David and Josh headed for the backyard with Clay's ball, figuring the 'Boys were in control, not even worried about maybe missing the start of the third quarter.

Josh was bigger than Clay or David, and had a lot of red hair that always seemed to be shooting off in different directions whether he'd just taken off his helmet or not. And he loved football the way they did, and Clay was sure he was on his way to being a star running back in high school, and probably college after that. He was strong and fast, and once he got going in the open field, got himself a good head of steam going, it took a pretty tough kid to take him on, head-on, and bring him down.

He also had an arm on him; everybody on the Stars knew it, the way they knew he'd rather use his legs.

But Clay knew you needed more than an arm to be a solid quarterback. Even if he didn't follow all college football as closely as he followed the Longhorns, he followed it closely enough to know that every single year a bunch of quarterbacks who could throw a football hard enough to put a hole in the side of a barn didn't come close to getting a job in the National Football League, most of them falling flat on their faces.

Or their butts.

Jalen King had also played some backup QB at practice, but when he was out there, Coach mostly had him run option plays because he had no arm at all.

So Josh was the best choice to replace David. And the problem, as both Clay and David were seeing now in the yard, wasn't how far he could throw a ball, or how hard. No. The problem was that he only knew where it was going about half the time. If that.

Clay had just gone out on a simple fly pattern, and somehow Josh managed to overthrow him by enough that the ball ended up in the woods.

A ball, Clay figured, that had traveled forty yards if it had traveled one.

While Clay went to retrieve the ball, David yelled out, "If that's the distance throw in Pass, Punt and Kick, I believe we've got ourselves a winner!"

"But if I can't put it in the same part of San Antonio as Clay, what does it matter?" Josh said.

"Because," Clay said when he got back with them, "we can show you how to throw it shorter. Nobody can teach an arm how to throw as far as you can."

"What we got to do," David said, "is just figure out a way for you to change speeds a little bit."

"You can do this," Clay said to Josh. "Think of it this way: If I can make Guerrero look good, I can do the same with you."

"Yeah, right," David said. "I guess that ball yesterday threw itself."

They went back to throwing short passes. David said the announcers were always talking about shortening the field. He said that for now, they just needed to shorten Clay's backyard. So they had Josh work on slants and quick outs and curls. David would stand right behind Josh and say, *"Now,"* when he wanted Josh to release the ball, often before Clay had even made his cut.

When he waited too long on a slant, David said, "Gimme the ball," before he grinned and said, "Making a couple of throws is *not* technically playing."

"No, sir," Clay said.

So he threw a quick out to Clay just as Clay was planting his foot for his cut. Then he had Clay run the same pattern and this time was lofting the ball even before Clay was into his move.

"No law passed against putting a little air under it sometimes," David said.

"You've got touch," Josh said. "I don't."

"You only think you don't," David said. "I'm just telling you there's more than one way to throw a football."

"I'm not a quarterback!" Josh said.

"For one game you are," Clay said.

Hoping against hope that it was just one game.

They were out there for nearly an hour. By then, Clay could see David running out of gas even though he'd done way more coaching than throwing. But the coaching he'd done had clearly helped out Josh before they finished. He was never going to read Clay the way David could, or know Clay's moves the way David did. But he knew all that a lot better than when he'd shown up. And had become a lot more accurate, even if they weren't confusing him with Aaron Rodgers.

They let him air it out one more time before they went back inside, and this time Josh laid the ball right in there, maybe ten yards before Clay got to the trees.

"Hey," David said when Clay came back with the ball, "let's not get *too* good."

"There's a lot of things I'm worrying on," Josh said. "Just not that."

David high-fived him. So did Clay. Clay handed him the ball and said, "Carry one of these around for the next couple of days every chance you get, fingers on the seams, like you're fixing to throw it."

The Cowboys-Redskins game was nearly to the end of the third quarter when they went back inside, the Cowboys having extended their lead to twenty by then.

"You feeling okay?" Clay said to David.

"Better now," he said, "now that Josh has gotten better."

Even with him hurt, they were still a team.


Clay didn't like to keep secrets from his parents. And he prided himself on never lying to them, not even about the smallest things. But he wasn't sure where the truth ended and a lie began when he left something out of the story.

And the story was that Coach had seen him walking on the

street and stopped the truck and the two of them had gone over to Olmos Park after that.

One of these days he would have to ask him mom or his dad or both of them if it was all right to stretch the truth a little bit to keep your word.

"Knowing Coach," his mom said, "he probably was on his way to check up on David and ended up hanging out with you instead."

Clay didn't respond to that, exactly, just said, "Glad he did."

"He's a nice man," Katherine Hollis said. "A sweet, wounded man." She sighed. "Sometimes he talks about having played football the way soldiers talk about having fought a war."

His dad had come into the kitchen then and said, "Hey, there's lots of similarities sometimes between sports and that whole band-of-brothers thing."

"Starting," Katherine Hollis said, "with the wounded part."

Clay managed to change the subject then, to the Longhorns, which was always safe ground for everybody, and didn't mention his visit with Coach again. And stayed away from it all day Sunday, before and after his workout with Josh and David, then through the four o'clock games.

Usually on Sunday nights, Clay would get to watch a fair amount of the *Football Night in America* game even though it was a school night, just because it started at seven thirty, their time.

If it was a really good game, his dad would give in and let Clay watch all the way to the end.

But he only watched the first half tonight because the Falcons were putting a good old-fashioned beatdown on the Colts, and

Clay wasn't all that interested in either team. So Clay finally told his dad he was going to call it a night and go upstairs and catch up on some reading before bed.

His dad's eyebrows went up so high Clay thought they might disappear into his hair.

"*School* reading?" his dad said. "During a Sunday night football game?"

"Nah," Clay said. "Football reading."

"Can I ask about what?"

"Coach's career," Clay said, and then told the whole truth about what had happened the night before. "We were talking some about it last night."

He headed up the stairs, ready to Google "Monty Cooper" again, wondering more than ever if Coach had to use the Internet to fill in the gaps on his own career, and his band of brothers.

# THIRTEEN

**F**UNNY THING WAS, CLAY PRIDED himself on his own memory.

He wasn't entirely sure how book smart he was, or would ever be, as hard as he worked to get good grades. But he felt like he had a good mind, one that could memorize page after page of plays in the binder Coach had given to all them, to the point where he was sure he knew the Stars' plays better than Coach himself did.

That part was a gift, Clay knew. He could look at a page, and it was as if his brain were taking a picture of it the way your phone could. It was just something that came second nature to him, like running or catching. He'd never really thought that much about it until lately, when his mom and just about everybody else on the planet who followed football started talking—and talking—about head injuries.

Now Coach was talking about getting lost, not just in his truck, but inside his own brain.

And Clay couldn't get any of this out of his own.

After he read back on some old stories about Coach, some of

them he'd read before—and hardly any of them talking about the concussions he'd suffered during his career—Clay typed out this on Google:

"Football players and memory loss."

The first thing that popped up was a story from the CBS News website, from 2015, that read this way at the top:

MEMORY LOSS TAKES TOLL ON FORMER NFL PLAYERS.

*Tell me about it,* Clay Hollis thought.

This is how the story started:

"National Football League players who suffered concussions serious enough to lose consciousness may be at risk for brain damage that can affect memory later in life."

Now they weren't just talking about brain wounds. Or the wounded, like his mom did.

Brain damage.

Like Coach's brain might be in worse shape than those old knees of his.

He wasn't just thinking about Coach, either, he was thinking about David, too, hoping David had been telling Doc Kellerman and everybody else the truth when he said he hadn't lost consciousness yesterday.

Clay wanted to stop reading, but didn't.

"Concussions," the story continued, "may damage the hippocampus."

It sounded like a school for hippos. Or animals that might be related to a hippopotamus. And would have been funny, thinking of it that way, like there was a part of your brain shaped like some fat hippo, except none of this was funny to Clay.

But now he wanted to know, so he read this part, too:

"The hippocampus is the brain's memory center. For reasons that are not well understood, a concussion—particularly when accompanied by loss of consciousness—causes this area of the brain to shrink, which in turn causes memory problems."

One of the doctors they talked to said this: "We are now beginning to understand that repetitive hits to the brain over time can be an important marker for mental impairment and memory loss, and potentially dementia or Alzheimer's."

The last word Clay knew, because Bryce Darrell's granddad had finally passed from Alzheimer's last summer. At the end, the Darrells had had to put him into a special hospital for people with that because he'd wandered away from his house and was gone for a whole day and night before they found him, because he hadn't been able to find his way home or even call anybody.

Clay closed his laptop and in a quiet voice said, "Great. Just great."

He remembered thinking it was crazy when that young linebacker for the 49ers, Chris Borland, had up and retired when he was still just twenty-four years old because he said he was worried about head injuries. Clay was only ten when that happened, but he remembered Bryce, already playing linebacker by then, saying that if a guy was afraid of getting hit, maybe he should go bowling, unless he was afraid of dropping the ball on his foot.

"That's plain old crazy, giving up football because of something you think *might* happen to you someday," Bryce had said.

Maybe not so crazy, Clay thought now, his laptop next to him on his bed. If Clay could look this stuff up, so could somebody like Chris Borland, and then talk to doctors himself, all the doctors he wanted. No, maybe he wasn't crazy to walk away from a game he surely must love the way Clay did.

He thought about going back downstairs and watching a little more of the game before he did get into bed for good. But his heart wasn't in it tonight. Head, either.

He washed up and brushed his teeth and turned out the lights and got under the covers. Sometimes having a memory like he had was no fun at all. Because even in the dark now, even with his eyes closed shut, he could still see the page he'd been reading.

Every single word.

# FOURTEEN

**T**HE STARS' NEXT GAME, THEIR first—and hopefully their last—without David Guerrero as their quarterback was against the Saints at St. Paul High School, between Balcones Park and the San Antonio Zoo.

The only way David could help them today was by standing next to Coach Coop, not officially acting as his offensive coordinator, but pretty much acting as his offensive coordinator. It was a good thing. They all knew that even though Coach had been an offensive player in the pros, he sometimes could get lost in his own playbook. Bryce Darrell said it was a show sometimes, listening to Coach think out loud while Clay and David and the guys were on the field, trying to decide what to do from one snap to the next.

"Even I help him out sometimes," Bryce said.

"Calling plays?" Clay said.

"Nah. But I'm *excellent* at down and distance."

When Coach spoke to the team before the game, his pregame speech was even shorter than usual.

"We all got one job today, apart from trying our hardest," he said. "We got to support our quarterback, who we all know will be trying his hardest." Then he turned to Josh and said, "We all got you today, hoss."

David whispered to Clay, "By the end of this game, Josh will think his name is *Hoss* Bodeen."

They had all seen what Coach had done during their two practices that week: He had kept the playbook, at least the part that involved their passing offensive, as simple as possible. He had Josh work on quick drops and easy reads and told them that if there was any doubt in his mind once he did drop back, to do what he does best, and pull the ball down and run with it.

"Hoss," he said now to Josh, putting an arm around his shoulder. "You don't need to play nobody's game today except your own. There's your game plan right there."

Then they all yelled, *"Go Stars!"*

Clay went over to take one last swig out of his water bottle, and David walked alongside him. "You know what our game plan should be today? Get a lead."

"And keep it."

"Now, that really does sound like a plan."

"How's your head?"

"Stop asking me that."

"Okay, last time: How's your head?"

"Filled," David said, "with x's and o's."

David might have been good at x's and o's, but it turned out that the game plan that he and Clay imagined for the Stars wasn't worth what Coach liked to call a bucket of spit, because by the end of the first quarter they were already down two scores.

• • •

The first Saints' score, off an interception, wasn't really Josh's fault. The Stars had been running the ball fairly well on the opening drive, Will Kellerman doing a pretty fair impression of Josh now that Coach had moved Will into the backfield. And Josh had run the ball a couple of times himself, keeping it instead of pitching it on the option, even if he'd missed his first two throws, both to Will, badly.

But Josh fumbled a snap pulling away from center too quickly, lost a yard. The Saints blitzed on second down, and Josh managed to get away from the first wave of tacklers, but still ended up losing four yards. So they were facing third and fifteen from the Saints' forty-yard line. Coach—or maybe it was David—sent in roll right comeback. Josh was to roll to his right, and Clay was supposed to take off down the sideline, like it was a full-out fly pattern, before putting on the brakes and coming back, making sure he was clear of the first-down marker.

Before they broke the huddle, Clay said to Josh, "I'll be there. You just lay it in there, and I'll take care of the rest."

"I haven't completed a single pass yet."

"You're gonna complete this one."

He should have. The cornerback covering Clay had given him way too much room, thinking Clay was going long. When Clay did slam on the brakes and start coming back for the ball, knowing he just had to get past the Saints' thirty, he heard the kid at corner yell, "Shoot!" from behind him. He knew he'd created more than enough space as he saw the ball coming right for him, a spiral that looked as if David could have thrown it.

He never saw the safety flying in from his right. At the last moment, as Clay was looking the ball into his hands, the safety laid out for the ball, somehow managing to get a hand underneath it and send it straight up in the air, like he was a setter in volleyball.

Now it didn't matter that Clay had beaten the corner cleanly. What mattered was that the kid, sprinting to get back into the play, was at full speed, when the ball fell into his hands. He went past Clay like Clay was standing still because he *was* standing still. It happened that fast. The kid was fast. It was like he had a running start on everybody on the Stars' offense, including Clay, nobody catching him as he went seventy yards for the score.

The Stars' stopped them on the conversion. It was still 6–0. When the Stars got the ball back, they went three and out. Now it was the Saints going on a long drive, running it mostly, their quarterback, Case Fowler, mixing in just enough passes to keep Bryce and the boys honest on defense. Case finally went right up the middle on a quarterback draw, huge hole, like the middle of the Stars' defense had disappeared. It was 12–0, and stayed 12–0 all the way to halftime. The only time the Stars had been past midfield was right before Josh had thrown his pick six.

Worse?

Josh still hadn't completed his first pass. He either held on to the ball too long or got rid of it too quickly. A player who had never shown any fear running with the ball, and hadn't today when he'd run with the ball. But when it was time to put the ball in the air, he looked as scared to Clay as a Little League pitcher acting as if he could never throw a strike again.

When they came off the field at the half—Josh having just

missed a wide-open Clay again on a simple crossing pattern—
Josh's head was so far down Clay was surprised he didn't trip
over it.

Clay didn't have to move very fast to catch up with him, Josh
looked like he might need an hour just to get back to the bench.

"We're gonna come back, wait and see," he said.

"With who at quarterback?"

"You, you chump-wit," Clay said, giving him a light helmet
slap, trying to sound more convinced than he really was.

When they finally did get to the bench, Clay saw David sitting
and talking with Coach, David doing most of the talking, Coach
listening and nodding occasionally.

When they were finished, David got up and walked over to
Clay, who said, "What was all that about, Mr. Coordinator?"

"I have coordinated a plan," David said.

"Care to share?"

"We're going to run even more options than we have already,
but start throwing off it," David said. "And we're going to give
those suckers on defense a different look."

"What kind of look would *that* be?" Clay asked.

David grinned.

"You are gonna *love* coming out of the backfield!"

"We don't have a single play that has me in the backfield."

"Well, we do now, cowboy."

"You're making up plays?"

"Like we're in your yard."

Now Clay grinned. "I like it. A different look."

"Then look out."

"You think it will work?" Clay said.

"Look at it this way," David said. "What have we got to lose?"

It worked.

Mostly it worked because it seemed to not only cross up the Saints' biggest and best player on defense, a kid named Brock Culpepper, but finally slow him down.

Brock was another one of those guys who really had no defined position. Sometimes he was in the middle of their 3–4, sometimes he lined up on the outside. On either side. Sometimes he dropped back and played safety. They'd even bring him in on offense sometimes as a second tight end, usually in short-yardage situations. A couple of times they even put him in the backfield and let him lead sweeps, where he'd look like a truck coming at you on an open stretch of road.

But he was far more valuable on defense, blowing up plays the entire first half, especially once he could see that Josh would much rather run with the ball than try to throw it.

Only now the different look David had talked about had Brock looking at Clay, who'd officially become Josh's wing man. On the Stars' first series of the second half, Josh rolled to his right the way he had plenty of times in the first, Clay out in front of him. But just when it looked as if Josh was making his cut upfield, he stopped. As he did, Clay broke hard toward the sideline. Josh soft-tossed him the ball. The pass didn't travel more than five yards. But Clay ran ten yards down the sideline after he caught it. First down. First completion of the game for Josh Bodeen. The Stars weren't on the board yet. But he was.

In the huddle he said to Clay, "Least I won't go my whole Pop Warner career without completing a pass."

"You're gonna complete a lot more today before you're through. You know what we really did right there? We got ol' Brock's attention."

Josh tipped back his helmet and smiled. It was the first time he seemed to relax—or exhale—the whole game. "Better you than me," he said to Clay.

Josh rolled out again on the next play, waited until the last second to draw Brock to him, then pitched it to Will, who ran for twelve yards, his biggest gainer of the day. Next play Josh stepped up and hit Clay on a quick curl. He looked up to see Brock closing fast on him. Too fast. Clay spun away and ran fifteen yards before being run out of bounds. They were at the Saints' twenty-five.

Some of the plays did have names they recognized from their binders. But sometimes Will or Rashad Dyson, the running backs bringing in the plays from the sideline, would just tell Josh to roll again and for Clay to get open on that side of the field. Or tell Marc Franklin, their tight end, to do the same.

At the twenty-five, with another first down, Rashad said to Clay, "David says you should run Porter and go."

It actually made Clay laugh.

"Porter and *go*?" Josh said.

Clay said, "The Porters are our neighbors. When we play touch football in the backyard, a big play is me faking toward the Porters' house and then hauling butt deep."

"Thanks for the translation," Josh said.

"Don't worry," Clay said, "it's good for a touchdown practically every time in my yard. So just pretend that's where we are."

Clay lined up in the slot this time. He took off as soon as the ball was snapped, running about five yards from the left sideline. Then he broke toward the sideline, felt the corner come up on him, crowding him too much for a change. And took off.

It wasn't the prettiest pass he'd ever seen, the ball wobbling like it was learning to fly. But it didn't matter, because Clay was that open. He slowed down, even came back a little at the five, collected the ball, ran into the end zone from there. It was 12–6. *Now* they were on the board. On the conversion, Josh faked it to Clay on the left side, found Marc all alone in the corner of the end zone on the right. It was 12–7. The Stars weren't just on the board. They were in business.

To Clay, it felt as if they really were making this one up as they went along, like they really were just having a game in the backyard. Maybe that was the way football was supposed to feel, if you thought about it.

The defense held the Saints. Their kicker practically whiffed on a punt, shanking the ball off the side of his foot. It went ten yards. The Stars took over on the Saints' thirty-eight-yard line.

On first down, Brock Culpepper finally introduced himself to Clay.

Big-time.

Big. Time.

# FIFTEEN

**T**HE PLAY *WAS* OUT OF the binder: "Eighty-Seven post." The only difference, Will said when he brought the play in, was that Clay was still supposed to line up in the backfield, then go in motion before the snap.

They were trusting Josh's arm now, because this was a down-the-middle throw into the heart of the Saints' defense. Will was already at full speed as Josh was dropping back. He gave a little fake to the outside, then broke to the inside. As he did, the ball was there. But so was Brock, who'd been spying Clay the whole time.

The ball hit Clay in the hands right before Brock hit him, knocking Clay off his feet, spinning him around. Helicopter deal.

Clay was flying.

Two things happened then, both good. The first was that he held on to the ball when he finally came crashing back to earth.

Better yet, he didn't land on his head.

What he landed on was the ball. Which took air he didn't even know he had in him out of his body. But before it happened, he had managed to get his hands underneath the ball, which never touched grass. The ref was right there, and could see, signaling good catch with both arms.

Then he looked down at Clay and said, "You okay, son?"

Clay nodded, and managed to get enough oxygen in him to say, "Yes, sir, just got the wind knocked out of me."

"And nearly all the stuffing," the ref said.

Clay tossed the ball up to the ref. Then Brock reached down and helped him up.

"How the heck did you hold on?" he said.

"Wanted to, I guess," Clay said.

Clay looked over to Coach and gave him a thumbs-up, then quickly did the same thing in the direction of the place in the stands where he knew his parents were. Coach still called a timeout, sent Maddie out with water.

"Coach thought maybe everybody could use a nice, quick rest," she said.

"Starting with me, right?" Clay said.

"'Specially with you, you chump-wit."

"That's my word," Clay said.

"With good reason," she said.

He drank some water and thought, You just get lucky sometimes. Sometimes you got lit up, and went down, the way David had. And sometimes you landed just right. Clay hadn't gotten his bell rung. Maybe it wasn't luck. Maybe it was just football.

Maybe he would have reacted differently if he'd known Brock was there. But he didn't. So all he did was react to the ball. Made the catch. Stuck the landing, even if it hadn't been pretty. He could still take a hit, from a hitter like Brock.

Clay always wanted to win, whatever game he was playing, whatever sport. It was the way he was wired, that's what his dad said to him one time, telling Clay he wished he'd been wired the same way when he was a boy. He always wanted it. But today he wanted it even more than usual. For David. Who *had* taken one for the team.

Now the team was going to take one for him.

The Stars ended up with second and goal on the seven-yard line. Will brought in the play this time.

He said, "We're gonna throw for it."

"I'm totally down with that," Josh said.

"Uh, just one problem with that," Will said. "Coach and David sort of want Clay to throw."

David was still making things up as he went along.

Will said, "Josh is supposed to pitch it to you, Clay. You run right with it, like it's a straight sweep. While you're doing that, Josh sneaks out around left end. David swears he'll be wide open in the corner."

Clay leaned out of the huddle and looked over at David Guerrero. Who smiled at him and then pointed to his own head.

Clay just shook his.

"Just curious," Josh said. "This another play you like to run in your yard?"

"Nah," he said. "David's."

You could say they ran it the way it was drawn up. Drawn up in David's imagination. And Clay's. Josh took the snap, turned and pitched the ball to Clay. Who ran right. Hard. Like the most important thing for him was getting to the edge, and then the end zone after that.

But just as he should have been planting his right foot and making his cut, he stopped. So did his blockers, because Clay had reminded every one of them in the huddle to not cross the line of scrimmage.

*"He's throwing!"* somebody from the defense yelled.

That's exactly what he was doing. Was he ever. To Josh, who was side-open in the left corner of the end zone. Before he'd released it, Clay had told himself not to baby the throw, to throw it like he meant it. He did. Josh caught it. First touchdown pass Clay Hollis had ever thrown in his life. It was 13–12, Stars. Rashad ran it in behind Marc Franklin for the conversion and it was 14–12.

It stayed that way deep into the fourth quarter. The Saints hadn't been able to move the ball, not really, for what felt like an hour of real time. Maybe more. A long drive for the Stars had ended when Brock had knocked the ball loose from Will Kellerman inside the Saints' fifteen.

Still 14–12 with two minutes and twenty seconds left, Stars' ball at midfield. Second down. The Saints had two timeouts left, but it wouldn't matter if the Stars could make one more first down. They ran Rashad for four yards. Saints called their first timeout. Then Josh kept it in the option for four more.

Saints called their last timeout.

Fourth and two, Saints' forty-two.

Thirty seconds left.

Clay didn't think Coach would risk a punt. Too many things could go wrong. If they went for it and didn't make it, Clay knew the clock would stop on the change of possession. But the Saints would still have to go sixty yards or so in around twenty seconds with no timeouts.

Don't look at it that way, he told himself.

They needed two yards and they'd get them and the game would be over.

Rashad came in with the play.

In a quiet voice he said, "Eighty-Seven post."

"What the *heck*?" Clay said. "David wants us to *throw*? Over the *middle*?"

"Wasn't David called it," Rashad said. "Was Coach."

Clay looked at Josh. "Listen to me," he said. "Give me one look and then pull it down. You'll probably make the first down easy."

Josh shook his head. "I can't go against Coach, Clay," he said. "Not even for you. You know me."

Clay did. Being a team man to Josh meant doing what the coach told you to do. Even now.

"You get open like you're s'posed to," Josh said. "And I'll throw it like I'm s'posed to. And the game'll be over. Okay?"

"Okay."

Clay got open, the way he'd been getting open all day. But it didn't matter because Josh led him by too much. Way too much. And threw the ball right into the arms of Brock Culpepper, sitting there in the middle of the defense.

And suddenly there was all this open field in front of him, all this green, as he took off straight up the middle. Man, he *was* fast.

But I'm faster, Clay thought.

Clay's momentum had been taking him in the direction of the Saints' bench when Brock caught the ball. It gave Brock about a ten-yard head start. Clay didn't try to make it up right away, tearing down the sideline, wanting to cut down the angle rather than just chase.

He saw Brock put a move on Josh, and dust Josh. Then Marc Franklin. But those moves took time.

And Clay was gaining on him now, cutting toward the middle of the field like he was running another post pattern. Just not running down a ball now. Running down Brock Culpepper before he could score the touchdown that beat them.

Brock was closer to the left sideline now. Somehow Rashad caught up with him. But Brock straight-armed him, put him on the ground, then cut *back* toward the middle of the field, head down, having to think he was in the clear.

He wasn't.

Clay was waiting for him. When Brock looked up, there he was, no time to make a move, no choice but to run him over.

Clay had no choice, either, to do anything except what they still told you to do in football, even now:

Stick his head in there.

There was no time to try to remember all the things they'd been taught the first week of practice about new tackling techniques, whether you played offense or not. Everybody had to learn about what was called Heads-Up Tackling now, and even watch a video, learn about rising up into a ball carrier as if you were throwing a couple of uppercut punches while keeping your head back.

You weren't supposed to launch, not that Clay was thinking about launching himself into Brock Culpepper. Coach had told them to pretend they were pushing a guy up a hill, but that they'd better learn, or pretty soon tackle football in Pop Warner would be touch, which was something else, he said, that people were pushing.

It was just a way, Clay thought, of sticking your head in there while holding it back at the same time.

No time to be afraid. Do what you were taught. Be a football player.

Somehow he put it on Brock Culpepper before Brock could do the same to him. Threw his arms up into him and hit the ball square with his right forearm. And felt it come loose, and fall away from Brock, and to the side. Saw where the ball was on the ground before Brock did and fell on top of it, just as he felt Brock on top of him. But it was too late.

Now the game was over.

The offense stayed out on the field for one play, in the victory formation, where it looked like the whole team was around Josh Bodeen as he knelt down. Stars 14, Saints 12. Final.

The players from both teams got into lines and shook hands. Brock said to Clay, "You got me good."

"Right before you were about to get us," Clay said.

"See you again."

Clay shook his head and said, "How about next year sometime?"

Then he went to find David.

"Why in the heck were we throwing the ball?" he said.

David looked around. "Lower your voice, okay?"

"Okay," Clay said. In a much quieter voice he said, "So why in the heck were we throwing the ball?"

David looked around again and said, "Because Coach thought we were behind instead of ahead."

Clay stared at him. "But then you told him we were ahead, right?"

David nodded. "I did."

"And he still sent the play in?"

David nodded again.

Clay said, "What did he say?"

"He looked at me and said, 'Who the heck are you?'"

"Like, who are you to question me?"

"Yeah," David Guerrero said to his best friend. "Go with that."

Clay's mom invited Coach Coop over for dinner when the game was over. Clay backed the invitation up by saying to Coach, "It'll be great. We'll eat fast and then watch football."

"Eat *fast*?" Katherine Hollis said. "Eat my world-class meatloaf *fast*? That to me sounds like some very slow thinking, young man."

"Sorry," he said. "What I meant to say, Coach, was that we'll savor every bite of dinner and then, if we're not too full, go watch football."

"Had your mom's meatloaf before," he said, "and hate to miss it. But my knees have been acting up even more than I'm used to today. So I'm fixin' to just go home and put my feet up and watch football alone tonight."

"Are you sure, Monty?" Clay's mom said. "We could eat as early as you want."

"I am sure, ma'am," he said. "And I have to tell you, the thought of missing one of your home-cooked meals is paining me right now as much as these knees. So I'm askin' for your forgiveness, and a rain check."

"Always," she said.

Coach turned then and started limping toward the parking lot. Both Clay and his mom watched him.

"Why do I feel so sad all of a sudden?" she said, putting a hand on Clay's shoulder.

"Oh, he's fine," Clay said, knowing that he really wasn't. "And cheer up, we just won ourselves a big game."

But she was still staring, watching as Coach heaved himself into the truck before it disappeared around the corner.

"You know what I wonder sometimes?" she said. "I wonder what his life will be like when the season is over, and he doesn't have football anymore."

"Hey," Clay said. "There's a long way to go before the end of the season. And look at what-all Coach has to look forward to."

"You boys winning him one more championship?"

"Well, obviously," he said, grinning at her. "And then after we do that, don't forget, Coach gets to be on the field with his old teammates on Thanksgiving."

His mom nodded. "You're right," she said, "I should focus on Coach chasing a couple more memories."

They were at home later, getting ready for dinner, when Clay's dad answered the phone in the kitchen and found out Coach had been in a car accident.

# SIXTEEN

A S SOON AS HE PUT down the phone, Ben Hollis said to them, "The good news is that he's not hurt."

"Thank God," Katherine Hollis said. "What happened?"

"The policeman gave me sort of a bumper-sticker version," he said. "Apparently, he decided to pick up some take-out food at Rosario's, and somehow cut over to make a right turn with his left blinker on, and got hit on the passenger side of the truck by the car he cut in front of."

"But he's okay for real?" Clay said.

"Policeman said he is," his dad said. "But he said there's a fair amount of damage to the truck, which he said can't be driven. Why we have to go pick him up. He asked them to call us. When they asked him our number, he told them to go through his contacts and look for 'Clay's dad.'"

In a quiet voice Clay's mom said, "Because there was no one else he felt like he could call."

Clay wondered whether Coach had just gotten confused. Or whether he'd forgotten where he was going, even if he'd set out to go to Rosario's. Lost or confused? Clay was starting to get confused, wondering if there was even a difference.

They picked up Coach at the police station. Clay didn't know what he was expecting. The policeman who had spoken to his dad had said that Coach was okay. And looking at him, it was hard to see anything other than a goose egg on Coach's forehead. Yet there was something in Coach's eyes that made Clay uncomfortable.

"You're coming back to our place for some home cooking," Clay's mom said. "The rest of that meatloaf's not going to eat itself. And this time I'm not taking no for an answer." She reached out a hand and placed it on Coach's arm.

"Dang it, Allie! I already told you I'm fine. Just get me out of this place."

Clay's mom looked like she'd received a shock from the carpeting. She slowly removed her hand.

"Who's Allie?" Clay whispered to his dad.

"Coach's daughter," his father said in a quiet voice.

"Of course, Monty," his mom said now. "We'll just get you home."

"Coach?" Clay said. "Are you sure you're okay?"

Coach trained his eyes on Clay and it was like watching a fog lift. Eyes that focused and suddenly understood. Coach shook his head in dismissal and said, "Course I'm okay. Just a little shook up is all."

Now those eyes met Clay's mom's. "What were you saying, Katherine?"

"I was asking if you were hungry," she said with a smile that looked a little sad to Clay.

"I don't want to be even more of a bother than I already am," he said.

"Friends don't bother friends," Katherine Hollis said.

They were silent on the ride home to Clay's, Clay wondering if Coach might have fallen asleep.

When they were inside, Clay asked if Coach wanted anything to drink and he said a soft drink would do him fine. Clay brought him a Coke and his mom brought a small ice pack, and ordered Coach to keep it on that bump until it was time to eat.

Clay sat with Coach in the living room while his mom cooked up some French fries and green beans to go with the meatloaf. He hunted around on the channel guide and finally found a pretty decent game, Auburn versus Ole Miss.

"You sure you're okay?" Clay said.

"I am now," Coach said, "though I'd rather just have ice in my drink."

Clay lowered his voice.

"You sure that knock on your head was the only place that got hurt?" he said.

Coach lowered his voice, too.

"Steering wheel gave me a little shot to the ribs, but I'll live," he said.

He leaned back, right hand holding the ice to his head, and fixed his eyes on the game just as a tall wide receiver for Ole Miss caught a deflected ball in stride, took off down the sidelines, and was gone.

"They always say that old ball will bounce funny on you,"

Coach said. "That's why you got to be paying attention." He winked at Clay. "You know what I always tell you boys about being alert, right?"

Clay grinned at him. "You're not paranoid, just *very* alert."

They both laughed, Coach laughing so hard he winced and put his free hands to his ribs. Then they went back to watching the game. When Clay's mom called in and said the food would be ready in five minutes, Coach said to Clay, "You didn't say anything to them about the other night, did you?"

If it wasn't Coach asking the question, it would have hurt Clay's feelings, Coach thinking he even had to ask him that.

"My word's good," Clay said.

"Know that," Coach said. "I just don't want anybody else worrying about me. Sorry that you have to."

"I don't mind," Clay said. "Worrying a little on you, I mean."

Coach was about to say something else, but then Clay's dad was walking into the room carrying a small tray table, his mom right behind with Coach's plate.

"What are you two worrying on?" she said to Clay. "How long it took me to prepare this feast?"

"Just getting our quarterback back on the field," Coach said, "is the only thing I'm worried about."

He made it sound like he believed that, even though Clay knew better. He had seen it at Olmos Park, and seen it tonight, the look on Coach's face.

The man who always preached that you couldn't play football scared was the one who looked scared now.

# SEVENTEEN

**I** WAS READING THIS STORY today," Clay's mom said as she was driving him to practice on Tuesday night.

This, Clay knew, was never good.

Lately, when she talked about reading a story, the story almost always had something to do with concussions.

He waited.

"It was in the *New York Times*," she said.

"You always make that sound like you're talking about the Bible," he said.

"Your father actually thinks it's the official publication of the devil," she said. "Anyway, it was about all those new tackling techniques that we read up on and watched videos about, the ones they put into play to make the game safer."

"And which won us a game the other day," he said, "when I separated Brock Culpepper from the ball."

"Well, I sure am glad it worked out for you," she said, "and for the team. But it turns out that those new techniques haven't made football any safer at all."

They were stopped at a red light. She gave him a quick sideways glance. "Turns out they sort of blew it when they told us all that Heads-Up Tackling stuff was the best thing that could ever have happened in youth football."

"Mom," he said, "that might be the only tackle I have to make all year."

"Not my point," she said.

"What *is* your point?"

He minded his tone of voice, because he didn't want her to think he was smart-mouthing her, or even debating her. If there was one thing Clay knew in his heart, it was that no one would ever be more on his side than his mom was. Or have his back more than she did.

"My *point*," she said, "is that there's not a whole lot more they can do to make the game less dangerous than it already is, which is why people are talking more and more about maybe outlawing tackle football until you get to high school."

They were at the field now. Clay looked out and saw he was one of the first to arrive. He was always one of the first. He loved football that much. He wasn't going to say it to his mom, but even with everything he'd learned about concussions and memory loss and all the rest of it, even with what had happened to David, he still loved it as much as he ever did.

He loved it even though he hated what it had done to Coach.

He started to get out of the car, but his mom put a hand on his arm.

"How would you feel about that?" she said.

"If they took tackling out?"

"Yes."

"Mom, I just want to play. I want to play and have fun. It's all I ever wanted to do. Isn't that what sports is supposed to be about?"

She reached behind her and handed him his helmet.

"For now, you're still going to need this," she said.

"Thanks, Mom."

"Do you think I'm trying to take the fun out of football?" she said.

"No."

*Yes,* he thought.

Before he closed his door, he leaned in and said, "Do you want me to stop playing?"

"No," she said.

"Then please just let me play," Clay said.

His mom gave him one of those smiles that had always felt to Clay like a hug.

"I love watching you play, pal," she said. "Just trying to use *my* head here."

One of the players who had beaten him to practice was David Guerrero, already in full uniform including helmet, despite the kind of late-summer heat in San Antonio that made you feel as if you were stepping into an oven set at a hundred degrees every time you stepped out of your house, or school.

Clay knew that David had had an appointment to see his neurologist at four thirty. David had said he was either coming straight to practice if the doctor cleared him, or going straight home to sulk.

But now here he was.

"You passed the test," Clay said.

"Aced the sucker."

"So you're back."

"*So* back."

"Your coaching career is over?"

"*So* over."

When Josh Bodeen got to the field and saw David soft-tossing with Clay, he let out a whoop.

"My parents always tell me that sometimes if you pray really, really hard, your prayers will get answered," he said.

"Oh, come on, you did fine Saturday," David said to him. "We won, didn't we?"

"Survived is more like it," Josh said.

Clay said, "What's Coach always say about wins? They're like his old girlfriends."

"All pretty," David said.

David's dad was putting them through their stretching drills while they waited for Coach Coop to show up. He said Coach had called and would be there as soon as he could, the guys at the body shop were just finishing with his truck.

When they did see Coach walking from the parking lot, carrying the binder with their plays in it in his hand, David said to Clay, "That was so weird what happened at the end of the game."

"It's like I told you after the game on the phone," Clay said. "It was just Coach being Coach. If he can forget our names, he can lose track of the score sometimes."

"In the fourth quarter of a close game?" David said.

"Probably never happen again in a million years," Clay said.

"You hope."

"And pray, just like Josh said," Clay said. "But, hey, if it does? He's got us."

Tonight he was the Coach they knew, joking around with them, even getting out on the field a couple of times and showing Clay—slowly—how to best run patterns out of the backfield, even showing him how to hide himself behind the tight end until it was time to make his move, either to the inside or outside.

This was the good Coach Coop, the best one, making Clay want to believe that maybe he'd just been going through a bad time and could fight his way out of it, just because nobody had more fight in him than the old Cowboy.

When practice ended he called the team into a big circle around him and said, "As you go through life, you're gonna find out what I found, sometimes the hard way, that you're never too old to learn, that you *can* teach an old dog new tricks."

Coach turned his head and Clay could see he was about to spit, until he saw that Bryce Darrell was right next to him. So he leaned over instead, and put a big gob near the old football shoes he wore, ones with the Cowboys' star on the heels.

When he looked back up he said, "Where was I?"

"Old dog," Clay said, "new tricks."

"Right," he said. "And what this old dog realized the other day that we got us a quarterback who knows the plays as well as I do. Maybe better. And a boy who can by-God make plays up as he goes along, almost like he's drawing them in the dirt at the playground."

"Got lucky, is all," David said.

"Wasn't luck at all," Coach said. "It was because you've got something up here"—he tapped his forehead with his index finger—"that I wish I had more of, which is smarts."

He took a deep breath and let it out, as if all this talking were tiring him out.

"Anyways," he said, "what I got through my own thick skull is that there's no call for me to *make* all the calls on this team. This isn't the dang NFL. I don't have to act as if my quarterback's wearing one of those fancy radios or whatever they are inside his helmet. Because I finally figured out my quarterback has enough of a head for football that he can start calling most of the plays his-self."

He turned and looked at David and said, "If that's all right with you."

"You mean it, Coach?" David said.

"I always mean what I say, son," he said. "There's more to teaching football than just teaching you how to throw and run and catch and block and tackle. You're gonna learn more about football this way than if we just keep running in one play after another."

He shrugged, and said, "Well, there you have it. See you Thursday."

Clay's mom had left a text message on his phone saying that she was going to be a few minutes late, and just to wait on the field. Coach said he'd wait with him, there was no place he had to be. So when the other players were gone it was just the two of them on the bench, Coach's binder between them. As they sat there, Clay felt the first hint of breeze he'd felt all day.

Coach placed his hand on the binder.

"That boy does know this book better'n I do," Coach said. "And I *wrote* the dang thing."

"He's only doing what you taught him, and seeing the game the way you want him to see it," Clay said.

Coach grinned. "You're a good boy."

"I always mean what I say," Clay said. "Just like you. And that's the truth."

They both heard the short burst of a car horn from the parking lot. Clay turned and saw his mom's car, her arm waving at him through the window on the driver's side.

"The truth," Coach Coop said. He really did sound tired now. "You know what the truth really is, son? It's like a hand of cards you got to play, whether you like the cards or not."

He made a face, and groaned, and stood up. Clay picked up his binder for him.

"Like 'em or not," he said.

The two of them slow-walked in the direction of the parking lot, Coach's hand on Clay's shoulder.

When they got home, Clay's mom showed him the picture of the two of them she'd taken with her phone.

"I know we talk a lot about football," she said. "But that moment right there, frozen in time? That's football, too. Almost made me cry."

Clay looked at the picture and knew exactly what she meant.

# EIGHTEEN

**W**ITH DAVID CALLING THE PLAYS, the Stars won easily on Saturday against the Colts at Holy Cross.

All week long the guys on the offensive line had said it was their mission to keep the Colts' defense off David, and that's exactly what they did. David went the whole game without being sacked and the only two times he ended up on the ground, by Clay's count, were when everybody was covered and he pulled the ball down and ran with it.

But Clay was open enough the rest of the day, catching two touchdown passes. Josh, back behind David, ran for another. Bryce and the guys on defense looked to be on a mission of their own, and ended up pitching a shutout. The final was 20–0. When it was over and they were in the circle, Coach smiled and said, "You boys could've coached your ownselves today."

When Coach was finished talking to them, Clay's mom invited him over for dinner. He said he couldn't, that he'd made other plans.

She said, "Do you have a date, Monty? Trying to make me jealous?"

"Just dinner with an old friend," Coach said, and left it at that.

"What was all that about?" Clay said when he was in the car with his parents. "Coach has turned us down before, but never because he had something else to do."

"It's a good thing," his dad said. "Nice to know that we're not the only friends he has."

It wasn't just that Coach had allowed David to call his own game today. He'd seemed a lot quieter than usual to Clay when the defense was on the field, even as well as their defense was playing. Bryce had stood next to him most of the time when the offense was out there. When the game ended, Clay asked Bryce if he thought Coach had been a lot quieter than usual.

"The only time he really said anything to me," Bryce said, "was when he told me to get out there."

"With us?"

"Yeah. All's I said back to him was that I'd just stay right where I was until it was time to go tackle somebody. Then all's he said was that he was just kidding around."

Maybe he was, Clay thought. Even if he wasn't, if that was the only time he got confused today, to Clay that almost felt like the team had won twice.

Later that night he called David and asked if he wanted to meet him at the Alamo in the morning, already knowing what the answer would be, but still knowing he had to ask him before he asked Maddie.

"I've already been there this year, you know that," David said.

"One time a year isn't enough," Clay said.

"You think one time a week isn't enough."

"Because it's not."

"Just because you're a history freak doesn't mean I have to be."

"You sure?"

"After church, I plan to veg until the football pregame shows."

"You mind if I ask Maddie?" Clay said.

"Go ahead," David said. "You two go have your Colonel Travis fun."

He texted her as soon as he hung up. Her answer—**What time?**—came so fast Clay wondered whether she'd been reading his mind.

Clay's mom drove them, and said she'd come back and pick them up when they were ready, she was heading over to the farmers market near the River Walk.

Clay and Maddie started at the Wall of History today, starting with the plaque for the Mission Period in the eighteenth century and then slowly making their way along the wall and through the years like they were traveling through time, Clay thinking that one thing never changed for him: Every time was like the first time.

"David didn't think it was weird, the two of us coming here?" Clay said.

"He might've, except we'd done it before."

"It was by accident that time."

She turned and smiled at him. She had her long hair in a ponytail today and was wearing a white Spurs T-shirt.

"So this is like . . . a date?" she said.

Clay knew she was playing, and smiled back. "There's no call for you to say mean things," he said.

A half hour later they were sitting in the shade, on one of the long benches in the Arcade, a long stretch of wooden beams over their heads, the wall behind them and across the way looking to Clay as if they were as old as the San Antonio River.

"David really didn't say anything," Clay said.

"You're stuck on this, aren't you?"

"Little bit."

"Basically, he looks at it as win-win," Maddie said. "He gets you off his back about the Alamo and gets me out of the house."

"C'mon, you guys get along great."

"Most times we do, but not all," she said. "Guys who don't have sisters don't understand brothers."

"He's like my brother."

"Try living with him."

They sat silently for a few minutes, sitting in this cool place, cool in all ways, the heat not so bad today. They had decided that before they left, they would hit the sacristy and the Long Barrack.

"Going to the sacristy is like going to church twice today," Maddie said.

"Just without the prayers," Clay said.

"Speak for yourself."

They were quiet again, until Maddie said, "I'm waiting."

"I thought we were taking a break," he said, "like this is halftime."

Maddie shook her head. "I meant I'm waiting for you to talk about whatever it is you got me here to talk about on our date."

"It's not a date and shut up."

"I'll shut up," she said. "You talk."

So he told her, swearing her to secrecy before he did, making her promise not to tell, but also telling her he knew she wouldn't.

Maddie said that it was lucky for him that he'd added that last part, because if he ever acted like he didn't trust her with a secret ever again he would have to find himself another Alamo friend.

Then she just sat and listened, not just her eyes focused on him, more like her whole self, as he told her about Coach and what Coach had told him at Olmos Park and how that plus what had happened at the end of the Saints game, Coach forgetting the score, had thrown a scare into him, and how Coach having even a minor car accident had just scared him more.

He said he'd been going back and forth on telling her, just because he had to tell somebody, but finally decided he wasn't breaking his promise to Coach, who'd said Clay couldn't tell his parents, or any of the other boys on the team, but hadn't said anything about the girl managing it.

"I just finally felt like my head was going to explode," he said.

"I know," she said.

"That my head was about to explode?"

"I know about Coach," she said. "Not about everything you just told me. But I know, even if I'm only eleven."

"You act older."

"Know that, too."

Then she was the one doing the talking and Clay was the one listening. She said that Clay might not notice sometimes, because he was so into the game, but she liked to stand near Coach, too, just because she loved football the way she did, and figured this might be the most time she was ever going to get in her life to stand next to somebody like Coach Coop, who'd not only played in the NFL but had played for her team, the Cowboys.

"He loses track of stuff all the time," she said. "And not just your guys' names." She grinned. "And mine."

"You never said anything to David?"

"Only after he called for that pass play against the Saints," she said. "Actually, David brought it up to me. But I said that it was Coach being Coach. And when he said he thought it was a little crazy, I said, 'Like Coach didn't act crazy before?'"

Clay said, "But do you think he's getting worse?"

Maddie shrugged. "He's like my grandma. She forgets things all the time. The only difference is, she's eighty-two."

"Coach isn't all that old."

"Nope," she said. "Nope, he's not."

Then she looked at Clay and said, "Football did this to him, right?"

"I think so," Clay said. "Not everybody who gets old and gets lost played football for a living. But, yeah, Mads, I think so."

"So what are we going to do?"

That sounded good to Clay. Her saying *we*. Like it was understood that they were now in this together.

"He basically told me he just wants this one more season," Clay said. "I was thinking on this the other night. He just wants to get back on that field in Dallas and celebrate that last title he won there. Before that, I think he wants to win himself one more title with *us*."

"I think you're right," she said.

"You sound surprised."

She put her hands out. "Boys are boys," she said.

Then she told him it was time for them to get moving, his mom wasn't going to stay at the farmers market forever and, besides, she did her best thinking when she was moving.

So they were moving again, through the monks' burial chamber and then their sacristy, through the Long Barrack. Maddie didn't say anything, so neither did Clay. There was chatter from the other visitors around them, Clay always thinking they were mostly tourists. Just not from them.

When they were outside, Maddie said, "I know what we have to do."

"Tell me."

"We're going to help him."

"Got it," he said. "But how?"

"The things he can't remember," Maddie said, "we'll remember for him."

# NINETEEN

THE PLAN, MADDIE SAID, WASN'T just to be Coach's memory. It was to be his brain, at least as often as they could manage.

"Like we're assistant coaches for his brain," she said.

"You actually think this can work?" Clay said.

They were back on their bench in the Arcade, Clay's mom having texted him and said she'd be there in about fifteen minutes. Then she was going to drop them at Maddie's house, so they could watch the one o'clock games with David. The Cowboys were the Sunday night game.

"Do I *think* it can work?" she said. "Yeah. Do I know it will? Heck, no. It's like football. We're just trying to make the right call here."

"But you *do* think it can work?"

"What I really think, in my heart of hearts, is that it can't hurt."

"We don't have anything to lose," Clay said.

"And if we don't do anything," Maddie said, "we might lose Coach for good."

They had talked some about how Clay might be helping Coach

out by telling his parents. But he honestly didn't believe Coach was in real danger, even after what had happened in his truck. And a promise was a promise.

"It's just another way of being a good friend," he said.

"Which to you is pretty much everything," she said.

"Not even pretty much," he said.

So the plan went like this: They'd sit down with Coach, the two of them, and convince him that the first thing he needed to do was get himself an iPhone to replace his old flip-top. Clay knew Monty Cooper would push back on that. Big-time. Clay could already hear him saying that he couldn't work the dang phone he already had.

"I can talk him into it," Maddie said. "I do it during games all the time."

"Like what?"

"Like, do you think before he let David call his own plays he was the only one calling them on the sideline?"

"You called plays?"

She smiled the kind of smile only girls can, like they know stuff you don't. And never will. "Maybe I did, maybe I didn't," she said.

They would not only get him to buy a new phone, they would teach him how to use it. Really teach him how. Not the bells and whistles, as Clay's mom liked to say when she was the one talking about how modern phones could do everything except cook Sunday dinner.

Just the basics.

Starting with him really learning how to use GPS once and for all.

They knew they couldn't program in every possible place Coach might go. But they could put in a whole bunch of places he liked to eat, whether he was eating at the restaurant or doing takeout. They could put in Clay's address and Maddie's, because Mrs. Guerrero would also cook for Coach sometimes. They could put in the gas station he liked to use, and his doctor's office, and AT&T Stadium, because Coach still took in some home games every year. They could show him, with the app called Waze, how easy it was just tap HOME when it was time for him to head home from wherever he was.

"We'll tell him that the nice lady voice giving him directions is just telling him how to run a pattern," Clay said.

"We'll tell him that lady is gonna be his new best friend," Maddie said.

The other thing they decided was that they'd program his phone and theirs so they would always know where he was, as long as he kept his phone turned on.

"You're trusting him to keep his phone charged?" Maddie said.

"I'm just trusting that we can make him understand that the only way we can help him is if he lets us help him."

"The best thing is, far as I can tell," Maddie said, "is that he doesn't go all that many places."

"My mom says it a different way," Clay said. "She says that Coach's world just keeps getting smaller."

At the start of every week, they'd ask Coach where he thought he might go on days when there wasn't football practice, or a Stars game. And Maddie would make up a calendar that he didn't even have to put in his phone, all he had to do was tape it to his refrigerator.

"We'll do everything we can to get him going in the right direction instead of the wrong one," she said. "My mom's always talking about being forgetful makes my grandma anxious. I think Coach is the same way."

"Is this like a Hail Mary pass?" Clay said.

"Don't think we're there yet," she said. "Call it third and long for now."

He turned to face her on the bench and put out his fist. She pounded it with hers. He looked up and down the Arcade then and was reminded again how just being here, being at the Alamo, somehow did make him feel better about everything.

Especially today.

"This can work," Maddie said.

"It *has* to work," Clay said. "I've been doing a lot of reading lately. It's not like Coach is going to get a whole lot better."

"What do they say on television?" Maddie said. "We're not looking to stop what's happening to Coach. Just to contain it."

"Like he says," Clay said. "You can teach an old dog new tricks."

"He's not dumb," Maddie said. "He's hurt. Like this is his last football injury, and it just turns out to be the worst one of all."

She smiled at him again. He smiled back. He put out his fist again. She pounded it again, a little harder this time. Maddie said she'd come up with more ideas, more ways they could help Coach out if he agreed to go along with them. Today, she said, was just a start.

"A good start," she said.

"Like a new season starting," Clay said.

He felt his phone buzz, pulled it out, saw the text from his mom telling him she was out front.

"Glad we had this date," Maddie said.

"It wasn't a date!" Clay said.

"Whatever it was, I'm glad you asked me," she said.

"Same."

They were a team now.

# TWENTY

**T**HEY WAITED UNTIL AFTER PRACTICE on Tuesday
to talk to Coach Coop.

Clay had told his mom to pick him up fifteen minutes
later than usual, there was some new stuff he needed to go over
with Coach. Totally true. David had to miss practice that night
because he had a follow-up appointment with his neurologist, who
was leaving for some kind of convention and could only see David
at six o'clock. So Maddie told her parents they didn't have to worry
about picking her up, Mrs. Hollis could give her a ride home.

When practice was over, Maddie collected the footballs and
put them in Coach's old canvas ball bag, then she and Clay waited
until all of the other players were gone.

"Got a little time for us, Coach?" Clay said.

"Got nothing *but* time now that we're done with football for
the day."

He was seated at the end of the bench, his legs stretched out
in front of him, absently rubbing his right knee. He gestured for
Clay and Maddie to sit down next to him. "Step into my office,"
he said.

They were both standing in front of him. "We're good," Clay said.

Coach looked at Clay, then Maddie. "Last time I saw faces that long, old Jerry Jones had called me up to his office to tell me they were releasing me."

"It's nothing like that," Clay said. "We don't want you to go anywhere."

"This is a good thing," Maddie said.

"Really it is," Clay said.

"Why don't you tell me what's on your minds, then," Coach Coop said.

Clay looked at Maddie. She nodded toward Coach, like telling Clay to go ahead. He took a deep breath, let it out.

"It's like this, Coach," Clay said. "I told Maddie what we talked about in the park that night, about you getting lost and all the rest of it. I didn't tell any of the other players, like you asked me not to, or my parents. Just Maddie, and she hasn't told anybody."

The words were spilling out of Clay. He felt that if he kept talking, really fast, no stopping, then Coach wouldn't have time to get mad at him, even though he was staring right at Coach, whose face was showing him nothing, not surprise, or anger. Nothing.

"Thing is, I just had to talk to somebody, because I want to help you and I couldn't figure out the best way, and Maddie is one of the smartest people I know. And not gonna lie, Coach, I'm glad I did because as soon as I did, she came up with a really good idea. To help you, I mean."

For this one moment, it was as if Maddie wasn't even there.

All of Coach's focus was on Clay, even if the only expression on his face was no expression at all.

Finally, he said, "Maybe there isn't any help for the way things are for me. And the way they're gonna stay."

Maddie said, "We don't think so."

"You don't, huh?"

Maddie straightened a little, standing her ground. "No, sir."

Clay said, "You're not mad?"

"At you? For telling?" Coach slowly shook his head. "The one who shouldn't have told is *me*. Because this is my problem, not anybody else's."

Now Clay said, "No, sir."

"How do you figure?"

"You're the one always saying that everybody on a team looks out for everybody else, right?"

"Is that what I say?"

"You know you do," Maddie said.

"Well," Clay said, "we're looking out for you now."

"What'd you find out," Coach said, "that they got one of those little chips somebody can install in my brain?"

"You don't need one," Clay said.

"Clay and I figure that you need a little help doing what you're always telling Bryce and the boys to do on defense," Maddie said.

"Which is?"

Maddie smiled at Coach now. It really was some great smile. "We're just gonna be around to help you fill in the gaps," she said.

"Gaps," Coach said to her in a soft voice, "sometimes feel as big to me as a big old Texas sky."

"We can do this," Clay said. "The three of us. Together." He grinned. "You just gotta want it."

"And I suppose that you're gonna tell me how the three of us *are* gonna make this game plan of yours happen."

"As a matter of fact," Maddie said, "we are!"


Now it was Maddie doing the talking. Or most of it. She told that the first thing was going to be Coach driving the three of them over to the Apple store at the North Star Mall on San Pedro so he could buy himself a new iPhone.

"I'd just as soon hang on to the phone I already got," Coach said. He patted the pockets of his jeans and added, "Which is in the truck right now."

"Where it can stay," Maddie said. "For the stuff we want to do with you, you're gonna need an iPhone. Everything your old phone could do, an iPhone can do better. And way more of."

"But I've seen the screens on those things when you-all are playing with them," he said. "It's like I'm looking at a menu in a restaurant and there's too many things I can order."

"We'll get rid of the stuff you don't need," Maddie said. "And the things we can't delete, you just ignore."

"Tried that with my second wife," he said.

"We're being serious," Maddie said.

Coach grinned. "Me too."

Maddie told Coach that he was going to love his new phone once he got the hang of the basics. Told him there was a way for him to track the phone, and for them to track him.

"If I get lost," Coach said.

"You're not going to," Clay said, wanting to believe that.

Maddie said, "In case you do, we'll know where you are and how to get you home."

Then Maddie told him about the calendar she was going to make for him, and how before he went to bed at night, he could cross out that day, and then know what he was supposed to do the next.

Somehow Maddie Guerrero made it sound like this was a great adventure Coach could hold in the palm of his hand.

They heard a quick blast of a car horn, and saw that Clay's mom had pulled into the parking lot. Time to go.

"You make this all sound so easy," Coach said, "but we know it's not for somebody whose circuits aren't wired the way they used to be."

"We know it's not easy," Clay said. "But that doesn't mean we can't do everything we can to make things less hard."

"You ever think about how you're gonna explain to your folks, *both* your folks, all this extra time you're gonna be spending with your old coach?"

"Actually," Maddie said, "I have."

Even Clay was surprised. They hadn't talked about that. "You *have*?"

"We're gonna say that I'm making a little movie," she said.

At the same time, Clay and Coach said, "About what?"

"About you," Maddie said to Coach.

Then she explained, to him and to Clay, that she'd just been given an assignment in English to not just write a paper about someone in her life she admired, but have some video to go along with it.

And that she'd decided she wanted to do hers on Coach Monty Cooper.

Coach sighed. "What a lucky boy I am," he said.

"I think you mean Cowboy," Maddie said.

# TWENTY-ONE

**D**URING THE RAMS GAME ON Saturday, Maddie stood next to Coach the whole time.

The story they came up with was that there was enough new stuff in their playbook that Coach wanted Maddie there with his binder, just in case he wanted to send a play in to David and the guys on offense from time to time, which he still did. And which made no sense sometimes. A pass when they should have been running. A run when they should have been passing. Just a couple of times a game. The other players still just wrote it off to "Coach being Coach." David would just say that Coach's play-calling had been a little wacky from the start, and just went with that. Clay and Maddie knew better.

"You just keep him in his lane," Clay said.

Maddie said, "It's hard to do that when you're not the one driving."

"You know what I mean."

She did.

They also figured out a way to get Bryce away from Coach when the Stars were on offense, just in case Coach did start to wander off. The idea was to move Bryce down to the other end of the sideline from Coach, telling him that he could see what the other team was doing from a different angle.

"You won't be my eye in the sky," Coach said. "I just want you to give me a different set of eyes for what those other boys are doing on D."

Bryce bought it.

"Coach must think I got some defensive genius in me," Bryce said.

Clay said, "Did he actually use the word *genius*?"

"It was implied," Bryce said.

"Did you just say *implied*?"

"We had to use it in a sentence in English the other day," Bryce Darrell said.

Stars versus Rams turned out to be a great game. By now everybody in the league knew that the Stars loved to air it out, including the Rams. Their quarterback was a tall left-hander named Jase Hawley, who had every bit as much arm as David did. And kept looking for ways to show it off.

The Stars got ahead two touchdowns early, one on a twenty-yard pass from David to Clay. But the Rams came back, Jase throwing two touchdown passes himself, both to his tight end. So it was 13–13 in the second quarter. The Stars went on a long drive then, David calling almost all of the plays, Coach only sending in one, a play that worked, a quarterback draw on second and short that went for fifteen yards. The rest of the time David was mixing passes and runs, finally hitting Will Kellerman on a wide-out screen to make it 19–13. Josh ran it in for the conversion. It was 20–13. Two minutes left. It was enough time for Jase, though, who scored on a quarterback sneak, threw another one to his tight end for the conversion. Twenty–all at the half. It felt as if they'd played a whole game already.

When Clay got to the sideline, he asked Maddie how Coach was doing.

"He was more quiet than usual," she said.

"But other than that he seemed okay?" Clay said. "That was a good call on the quarterback draw."

"Uh, that was all me," she said.

"You sent that play in?" Clay said. "What did Coach want to run?"

"Don't ask," she said.

All Coach said to the Stars before the second half started was this: "Hope you're having as much fun playing this game as I am watching it."

Halfway through the fourth quarter the Stars went back ahead, 27–20. Coach had sent in just one play on the scoring drive, a pass to Clay out of the backfield that got the Stars a big first down. Clay wondered whether that was Maddie, too, and what her brother would think if he knew his kid sister was calling some of the plays.

It was David who put Clay back in the slot and hit him for the conversion pass that put them ahead. But Jase came right back again, needing just five passes to take the Rams down the field, then running it in himself for the extra point. And they were tied again, 27–27.

They had lost one game already. Clay didn't think that two losses would knock them out of any chance to make the playoffs. But he didn't want the Stars to get a second loss this early in the season, especially in a strong league.

Two minutes, thirty seconds left in a game that was right there, waiting for them to take it, maybe not even give Jase Hawley a chance to get the ball back.

Before the offense went back on the field, David said, "How do you want us to play it, Coach? When do we take a shot down the field?"

"Play to win," Coach said.

"That's it?" David said. He shot a quick sideways glance at Clay, who shrugged.

"Is there ever anything else?" Coach said.

"No, sir," David said.

David and Clay started to run out on the field. Coach put a hand on David's arm.

"So how do you think we should play it?" he said.

David said, "Start off with short stuff, then take a shot down the field first chance we get."

"And play to win," Coach Coop said.

The Stars started out at their own thirty-eight. David put Clay back in the slot, called for one of the new plays in the binder, slot curl. Clay was to follow Marc Franklin, their tight end, as Marc angled toward the sideline. Then as soon as Marc did make his break in that direction, Clay was supposed to make a quick cut

into the middle of the field, even moving back toward David a
little. Play worked just the way it was drawn up. Ball was right
there, just ahead of the Rams' safety, who put Clay down. Hard.
He felt some pain in his side. Nothing major. Just football. Tackle
football. Take the lick, hold on to the ball, get up, do it again.

It was funny, Clay thought as he ran back to the huddle, knowing the clock was running:

No hard hit bothered him these days as long as it wasn't a hard
hit to his head.

Gain of eight. Plenty of time. Josh ran for the first down. David
still didn't need to use his last timeout. Just under two minutes.
David crossed the Rams up then. They dropped back one of their
linebackers, expecting a pass. David handed it to Josh again. He
ran for ten yards, and now they were in Rams' territory. David
said, "We're gonna use all this clock. We *ain't* giving Lefty the
ball back."

Clay said that worked for him.

They were under a minute and at the Rams' thirty after David
hit Clay on the sidelines and he got out of bounds. David was
looking over at Coach before they huddled up. Coach just stood
there next to Maddie with his arms crossed. Maybe it was his way
of saying it was their game. Or maybe he knew David Guerrero,
even at twelve, was doing just fine calling it. Maybe better than
he could.

David was into it now. They all were. But Clay knew his friend,
knew he loved using his football brain as much as his arm. Loved
the way he'd been thinking them down the field, using his brain
as well as his arm. And he sure wasn't playing afraid or worrying

about getting rid of the ball too soon because of his concussion. He was standing in there, sometimes until the last possible second, waiting for Clay or Will or Marc or even Josh to break free. Sometimes in football, you only remembered the stuff you wanted to remember.

David completed a short pass to Marc over the middle, for five. Forty seconds left. Now David called his timeout. Maddie started out with water. David waved her back.

"Know we'd be leaving their quarterback with a little time if we score now," he said. "But let's score now."

Clay said, "And Bryce thinks he's a genius."

David looked at Clay and Will and said, "Pump and go. To whichever one of you is open."

"Love it," Clay said.

It was one of his favorite plays. Clay and Will both ran the sidelines, at about half speed, looking back at their quarterback after about ten yards, hoping they could get the guys covering them to do the same. Then David would pump-fake for all he was worth.

And then Clay and Will both tried to outrun their corners, hoping they would be the one to take the ball all the way to the house.

The kid covering Clay didn't bite. The kid covering Will did. Clay watched from all the way across the field as Will broke into the clear and David gunned the ball to him.

Right before David got buried by the defensive end coming from David's right.

But the throw was perfect, Will not even having to slow up for it, the ball falling into his hands at about the five, nobody close enough to touch him as he ran into the end zone. It was 33–27. Clay started to run for Will, but something made him look back to see if David was on his way toward the end zone, too, sprinting for Will the way he always sprinted for Clay after he'd been the one to make a catch like that, and a score.

Only David was still down.

*No,* Clay thought.

*Not again.*

He made a short cut and ran for David instead, not knowing what he would do if he was hurt again. If he'd hit his head. Again.

He wasn't hurt.

Oh, he was still on his back. But he was smiling, squinting up into the sun, coughing slightly.

"Taking a rest?" Clay said.

"Felt like I was swallowing my mouthpiece there for a second," he said. "Getting hit by that boy was like getting hit by a mule."

Clay reached down and jerked him to his feet, giving David's helmet a little slap with his free hand.

"How we doing up there?"

"Gorgeous," David said.

"So you didn't see how the play ended?"

"Didn't have to," David Guerrero said.

Now he slapped his own helmet.

"Saw the whole thing up here," he said.

# TWENTY-TWO

**A**FTER THE GAME, CLAY TOLD his parents that he and Maddie were taking Coach to the Apple store, saying they'd finally convinced him that it was time for him to retire his flip phone once and for all. And he told them that they might hang around with Coach afterward, because Maddie had this project going in English and that he'd offered to help her with it, since no one knew more about the life and times of Monty Cooper than he did.

"Maddie says she might use a real videocam later," Clay said. "But for now she's just going to video him off her own phone."

"Sounds to me," Clay's mom said, not knowing how right she was, "that you and Maddie have turned Coach into your own personal project."

"Little bit," he said.

"Hey," she said, "if it gives him something to do and feel a little bit less alone when he's not coaching football, fine with me."

"He needs more than football," Clay said.

"Maybe he always did," Katherine Hollis said.

"Sometimes I look at him and think that it's still the only real friend he's got."

"But he's got us," she said. "And he's got you. And now Maddie."

"Yeah," Clay said. "He does."

On the ride to the store, Coach Coop kept saying that he couldn't believe he'd let them talk him into this, all he was doing is wasting money and time on a gadget he was never going to figure out no matter how much teaching they did.

"Gonna tell you a little secret," Coach said. "I was never good with any kind of teaching if it didn't involve making me a better player."

Maddie said, "I think you forgot to remind us again that you can't operate the phone you already have."

Clay giggled.

"Go ahead, laugh," he said. "But it happens to be true. To me this is like takin' somebody who can barely ride a bike and askin' him to drive one of those fast cars at Daytona."

"I'm eleven," Maddie said. "Clay's twelve." She held up her phone. "And we can drive these babies."

"I was happy with rotary phones!" Coach said.

Clay asked what a rotary phone was. Maddie informed him it was the kind that people dialed, back in the day. It was just one more thing she knew that he didn't.

"Yeah," Coach said. "Back in my day. A day that made me very happy, by the way."

He managed to keep his complaining to a minimum at the store while a nice salesgirl showed him his new phone, transferred all the information on his flip phone to it, not that there was much information to transfer. Clay had seen that Coach had maybe a dozen phone numbers in his list of contacts, and half of them were restaurants where he got his take-out food.

The first name on the list was "Allie."

His daughter.

When the salesgirl asked what kind of case Coach wanted, Maddie didn't give Coach a chance to answer, just quickly said, "I'll pick one out."

The girl smiled at Maddie. "So I guess there's no point in me asking him about a screen protector?"

"We'll take one," Maddie said.

"Do you want me to put it on?" the salesgirl said.

"I got it," Maddie said.

Maddie went to pick out the case; the salesgirl went to get the screen protector. Coach called after them, "The other extra I'll need is somebody to walk around with me all day and operate this sucker."

He paid up when they were finished. He said he didn't want Apple Care, but Maddie explained why it was better to have it than not have it. Coach muttered something to himself that Clay thought might have cost him more money in his swear pot at practice, but said, fine, put him down for Apple Care. At one point he looked over at Clay, who was just smiling at the show.

"Something funny I'm missin' here?" Coach said.

"No, sir!" Clay said. "Just thought of something Bryce said during the game."

"That's what I thought," Coach said.

Coach was the first one out the door, on his way to the truck, still muttering. Maddie leaned close to Clay and said, "We having any fun yet?"

Before Clay could tell her he was actually having a great time, Coach's head snapped around and he said, "I heard that, girl."

Maddie whispered to Clay, "He just calls me that sometimes 'cause he can't call me hoss."

"Heard that, too," Coach said.

Clay didn't know what to expect from Coach's apartment but was pleasantly surprised when he let them in.

It was neat, for one thing. Really neat. And smaller than he'd expected, though, with Coach living alone, he didn't expect it to be all that big. There were two chairs in the living room, and a small leather couch, a big TV screen mounted on the wall across from the couch. Along one of the other walls was a long table, looking to Clay like some kind of antique even though he wasn't all that sure about antiques other than some stuff his mom's parents had given her for their living room.

The whole length of the table was covered with photographs, from when Coach was a player, behind a whole row of pictures of his daughter, Allie, from all different ages of her life. The last few had Allie posing with a man Clay figured had to be her husband, and Coach's grandson. Those had a whole lot of ocean in the background.

"Where do they live, your daughter and her family?" Clay said, pointing to the pictures.

"Maui," Coach said. "So far away it might as well be the moon, just with beaches and palm trees." He handed Clay a postcard with a glowing sunset. Clay turned it over and saw a short message in neat, cursive writing.

"But you've been, right?" he said, handing the postcard to Maddie.

Coach nodded. "Last time was after the boy was born." He smiled, maybe at the memory of that. "She gave him Montgomery as a middle name, after me. I wasn't even sure Allie knew that was my God-given name until then."

Coach turned on the television, almost as if doing it by force of habit, to one of about a hundred games that were on every Saturday afternoon. "Always put it on as soon as I walk in," he said, almost to himself. "Makes the place a little less quiet."

But Maddie asked him to mute it, because she wanted to show him how "Find My Friends" was going to work. When she was finished with Coach's phone, and her own, she asked Clay to hand over his.

She even showed Coach, on his phone and hers, how to use FaceTime.

"Why in the world do I need to see the person I'm talking to and have them see me?" Coach said.

"So the next time you talk to Allie on the phone, you'll be able to see her and your grandson," Maddie said.

"It'll probably be just one more thing I'll mess up with her."

"No, it won't," Maddie said. She smiled at him again. "After we work on your phone today, maybe we need to work on your attitude."

Then she made him practice a little more with FaceTime, even though they were sitting on the same couch.

"This is silly," he said. "You're right here next to me."

"What would be silly," Maddie said, "is if you didn't use this with your family."

She looked around and said, "Where's your laptop?"

"It's in the little room that's supposed to be a second bedroom, but I use as my office," Coach said. "Some old Dell I bought and don't use all that often."

"Next time we'll get you up and running on Skype," she said, and at that point Clay just said, "Baby steps, Mads."

Then Maddie started putting Coach's addresses into Waze, which she said was the best GPS system to use when he was going out in his car. All he'd have to do is scroll down before he took off in the truck and click on the address he needed.

Clay watched, actually surprised that Coach was letting Maddie coach *him* this way, more interested in them than the Ohio State–Illinois game he was about half watching. While they worked, Clay asked if he could see the office, and Coach said there wasn't much to see, it was the one part of the apartment full of clutter. Clay said, "You ought to see my bedroom."

It was in the small office that Clay found the scrapbooks, on a coffee table next to the desk with Coach's laptop on it.

There were two of them, thick, faded leather covers on them, one on top of the other. Clay moved some newspapers off the small couch and sat down and put the top scrapbook on his lap, and opened it up, not knowing it was like opening up the story of Monty Cooper's football life.

These weren't the kind of stories Clay had pulled up on the Internet. These were clippings and photographs from newspapers, page after page of them, the pages covered by plastic—to preserve them, Clay figured, keep the clippings from being more yellow than they already were—and taking Clay all the way back to when Coach was in high school.

From the other room, Coach said something Clay couldn't quite pick up and then he heard Maddie's laugh. But in here there was only the hum of the air conditioner and the sound of Clay turning the thick pages in the scrapbook, going through Coach's career, game by game and year by year. This was different from being at the Alamo. But Clay could still feel the history, almost as if it were speaking to him the way those old walls did when he'd walk along them on another one of his visits to Colonel Travis and the boys.

This was Coach's life. This was his history. Stories about him scoring the winning touchdown in this game or that. Pictures of him goofing around with his high school teammates or posing with one of the cheerleaders or hugging a trophy. Looking so young Clay almost couldn't believe it.

And smiling. Always smiling.

Clay had opened the second book, had gotten to the pictures and stories about Coach's years with the Cowboys, when he heard Coach call to him from the other room.

"That room isn't big enough for you to get lost in," he said.

"Got lost in your scrapbooks, Coach," Clay said.

"Those old things?"

Clay carried the one in his hands out into the living room and said, "Did you start keeping these?"

"Was my mama," Coach Coop said. "She took me all the way to my second year with the Cowboys, which is when she passed. That's why the first one is better organized and easier on the eyes than when I took over for her. But those books were important to her, so they became important to me, too. She used to tell me, before there was an Internet or any of the rest of it, that someday it would be important for me to have my memories all in one place."

He lifted his shoulders and let them fall, just a little bit of a smile on his face as he said, "Little did she know."

Clay said, "Mads, you have to make these scrapbooks part of your movie about Coach."

"Done," Maddie said.

She said they were almost done with Coach's phone. Clay went back into the office and finished looking through the rest of the second scrapbook. A picture of Coach with Troy Aikman. Coach blocking a kick to win a game when he was a rookie, against the Giants. Coach standing between Jerry Jones and Jimmy Johnson. A story about the friendship between Coach and Michael Irvin. The headline on that one was, TEXAS STADIUM ODD COUPLE.

There was a small story, stuck at the bottom of the page, just a couple of paragraphs, about Coach missing his first game with the Cowboys, in his third season, because of a concussion suffered the week before against the Cardinals. Knowing what he knew about concussions by now, everything he'd learned, Clay just knew it must have been some concussion for Monty Cooper to finally have to take a Sunday off.

Most of the pages at the end of the second scrapbook were filled with stories and pictures about the blocked punt that had put the

Cowboys into their last Super Bowl, at least for now. That was the Cowboys team that would be honored on Thanksgiving with the whole country watching. Coach had been part of other Cowboys teams that had won Super Bowls in the 1990s. But he'd already said the last one was most special, because he'd had the biggest hand in that one, in all ways. And maybe because the Cowboys hadn't been back to the big game since.

The second-to-last page was mostly taken up by a photograph of Coach hugging the Vince Lombardi trophy after that game against the Steelers for all it was worth. Underneath it was the story about the Cowboys releasing him, Jerry Jones saying that that last knee surgery was "just one dag-gone surgery too many, even for somebody as tough as ol' Monty Cooper."

The last line of that story was Jones saying that Monty would be a Cowboy forever.

The last page was just a picture of Coach's helmet, looking as if it had taken some beating, with the famous Cowboys star on the side. But pasted alongside was a yellowed newspaper clipping with tiny print. A birth announcement.

*June 14, 1990. Allison Clara Cooper*
*at 2:12 a.m. to Mr. and Mrs. Montgomery Cooper.*
*7 pounds, 14 ounces.*

Clay suddenly felt like he was spying on something private. He quickly closed the scrapbook and walked back into the living room.

"Learn anything?" Coach said.

"Yeah," Clay said. "You were even better than I knew."

"On that team?" Coach said. "Heck, on that team we had back in the nineties, it was hard *not* to look good. If we hadn't had one nightmare first quarter in San Fran one time, we would've been the only team in pro football history to win four Super Bowls in a row."

"There's still plenty enough history in those books."

"Ancient," Coach said. Then he turned to Maddie and said, "We done here, girl?"

"Done with the phone," she said. "Hope I didn't wear you out too much that you can't answer a few questions for what is going to be my brilliant movie."

"How about we start that next Saturday?" Coach said. "You told me you got some time, right?"

"I do," Maddie said. "Next week it is."

Then she asked Coach if he had some Magic Markers. He told her he was pretty sure there were a couple in the top drawer of his desk. She asked him about some copy paper and he said there ought to be some in his old printer, if he hadn't run out and forgotten to replace it.

Maddie headed for the office. Coach and Clay watched some of the Ohio State game. When she returned, she showed him his first weekly calendar, pointing out that the only thing he had to remember other than football practices and next Saturday's game was a trip to the doctor Coach had told them about; he said he needed one more MRI on his right knee, the one that had been bothering him the most, though he said sometimes it was hard to tell which knee was winning that particular competition.

"More dues," he said.

Maddie asked for the doctor's name, and Coach told her not to worry about it—he'd put the address in himself—it would be a nice little test to see if he'd learned anything at all today.

"You promise?" Maddie said.

"Cross my heart," he said.

"To be continued," Maddie said.

"Do I have a choice?" Coach said.

Maddie looked at Clay. They both looked at Coach and shook their heads. But when they were all outside, on their way to the truck, Coach said, "Thank you. Both of you."

"You don't have to thank us," Clay said.

"Just did."

"Well then," Maddie said. "You're welcome." She grinned. "Coach, you're not the only one who learned something today. I did, too."

"And what's that?"

"I like coaching!" she said.

Coach stopped then, put one hand on Clay's shoulder, the other on Maddie's.

"I won't forget this," Coach said.

This time Clay believed him.

They left and piled into the backseat of Mrs. Hollis's car. Before she even clicked her seat belt on, Maddie handed something to Clay.

"What's this?" he said.

"A postcard. Something to remember the day by."

# TWENTY-THREE

LATER THAT NIGHT, THE DOOR to his bedroom closed, Clay called Maddie.

"I forgot to ask you," he said. "How did you pull that idea about Coach and the movie out of your pocket?"

"Glad you said pocket."

"Seriously," he said.

"I thought of it one second before I said it," she said. "I'd been trying to come up with a good idea for my project, and it just popped into my head. Almost like I called an audible!"

"What's Mrs. Sullivan going to think?"

Mrs. Sullivan had been Clay's English teacher last year, was Maddie's this year.

"I already emailed her, and she loves it, because she knows how much I love football. She said it's almost a combination of English and history."

They talked a little more about their day with Coach after that, what it had been like watching him try to work his new phone with his old, crooked fingers. But how happy he'd been when he did something right. Happy and relieved.

"You know what it was like today?" Clay said. "It was like Coach trying to convince himself that if he really, really concentrated, he could get his mind to work like it used to."

"Maybe it's not as bad with him as we think," Maddie said.

"I keep telling myself that."

"Hey, it is what it is," Maddie said. "We're just gonna have to work with what we have."

Clay didn't say anything then. Neither did Maddie. Finally he said, "You think if our parents knew what we know they'd be making Coach go see a doctor, maybe like the one David had to go see after his concussion?"

"Like maybe there's some pill or medicine he could take?"

"*I just don't know!*" Clay said, the frustration just shooting out of him.

"I know," Maddie said, her voice sounding like a whisper compared with what Clay's had just been.

Clay said, "I've learned so much this season about what football can do to you, what it did to Coach. But I have no idea if there's any way to slow it down."

"You don't think Coach has tried to find out for himself?"

"He's pretty stubborn, even when you're trying to help him."

"Hadn't picked up on that," Maddie said.

"You know what he says on the field," Clay said. "'Control what you can control.' We just need to be stuck on that and on getting him through the season."

"We have to," she said. And then Clay said, "You know, Mads, I was thinking about something tonight. I still love football. I do. But with everything that's going on, it's hard sometimes to think about it the way I used to. Does that make any sense?"

"A lot."

Then she laughed and said that she couldn't think about him thinking about football right now, she wanted to go watch it, Alabama was playing Mississippi State.

"Same," Clay said.

He said he'd call her tomorrow, as if calling her two days in a row was suddenly the most natural thing in the world. But then it seemed sometimes as if he and Maddie'd had two seasons going right now, one on the field and one off it.

Both important.

The Stars kept winning, just the one loss on their record, still tied for first place. Clay couldn't believe how fast it was all going, even with everything that had happened so far, with what he'd had to overcome early in the season, with what had happened to David, what was going on with Coach.

Somehow they were into October now, getting closer to the end of the regular season.

They'd known the deal all along, that the top four teams in the league made the playoffs, their league's version of the Final Four. The championship game, if they made it that far, was scheduled for the Saturday before Thanksgiving.

So if everything worked out the way Clay wanted it to, if he got the ending he wanted, Coach would get one more big day, one more title game, with the Stars. Then a few days later he'd get an even bigger day in Arlington with his old teammates, coming out of the tunnel with them one more time. Hearing himself introduced one more time as a Cowboy—a Cowboy forever—and then hearing the kind of cheers he used to hear.

The Stars just had to keep it together for another month. So did Coach. It was weird, when Clay really thought about it. He'd started out the season with one dream in football.

Now it was like he was chasing two, with four regular season games left, starting today with the Buccaneers, who were tied with the Stars in first place.

In Pop Warner it wasn't as if you got the chance to scout your opposition. Everybody played on Saturday. Nobody got a Saturday off. And it wasn't as if there were some weekly Pop Warner highlight show you could watch in San Antonio.

But you heard stuff. And they had heard how good the Bucs were and had followed them as much as possible on Instagram. Clay and David and the guys knew by now that when the Bucs had suffered their one loss, it was because their quarterback, Mac Sherrill, had been sick with the flu.

From everything they'd heard, Mac was one of the Bucs' two best players. The other was one of their safeties, Willie Sharpe, who also played some wide receiver for them. And returned kicks. And even punted. The way the other kids in the league talked about Willie on Insta, he was about the fastest thing this side of Usain Bolt. On top of that, he was supposed to hit like a middle linebacker.

"I don't care what other guys say about him," David said as

they watched Willie and his teammates warm up at the other end of the field at Medina Valley High. "He can't cover you."

"And you know this by watching him *stretch*?" Clay said.

"What I *know*," David said, "is that since nobody in the league can cover you, he can't either."

"Tough to argue with logic like that," Clay said. "And, hey, he'll only be helping. The guy I have to worry about is whatever corner's on me."

"Yeah, but they're going to want to have their best going up against our best as often as possible," David said. "Dude? If we know about Willie, Willie knows about you."

"Today feels like a playoff game," Clay said.

"Today and every day," David said.

Coach told them pretty much the same thing in his pregame talk.

"When I was still playing," he'd said, "we used to call games like this midterm exams, whether they fell smack-dab in the middle of the season or not. They didn't determine the final grade. But they sure gave you an idea about what that grade was gonna be."

He paused and tried to take in as many faces in the circle around him as possible.

"By the way?" he said. "There's a good chance we might see these boys down the road. So how's about we give them something to remember us by if we do."

Coach hardly ever raised his voice. But he looked fired up now all of a sudden, as fired up as Clay had seen him all season long.

"*I want this one!*" he yelled. "*Who feels the same?*"

"*We do!*" the Stars yelled back at him.

It was the same today as it had been the past few games:

David called most of the plays. Bryce would take his place at the opposite end of the sideline from Coach, scouting the Bucs' defense from there.

Maddie was next to Coach.

She said there had been a few times over the past month when he'd gotten confused, and she had to help him with down and distance, even one time with what quarter it was. She said twice during the Dolphins game the week before, he'd forgotten that the Stars were ahead. The week before that, he'd turned to her one time and said that it was time to get Josh running with the ball again.

"Josh is doing just fine," she'd said, initially thinking he was kidding.

He snapped at her, "What game are you watching, girl? We haven't run our quarterback one time the whole game."

Maddie had told him, as gently as possible, that Josh was back in his regular position, and that Coach had put David back in at quarterback.

"Course I did," Coach said. "I was just testing my assistant coach."

And Maddie had said, "Course you were. You think I don't know when you're messing with me?"

She knew he wasn't messing with her. Maybe he knew, too. It was almost, Maddie had told Clay, like it was a game they were playing within the one they were both watching.

"Don't you ever tell him I said this," Maddie had said. "But everything that's going on has made me love him more than I ever did before."

Clay told her he knew exactly how she felt.

But what he really loved today was being in this kind of game against Mac Sherrill and Willie Sharpe and the Bucs, who were turning out to be as good as he had heard.

So were the Stars.

They scored first, Josh Bodeen breaking what looked to Clay to be about six tackles on his way to a thirty-yard touchdown run. After Willie Sharpe broke up a conversion pass to Will Kellerman, it was 6–0.

Mac Sherrill, though, came right at them when he had the ball, driving the Stars' defenders crazy on option plays, keeping the ball more often than not, usually waiting until third down to put the ball in the air. It was what he finally did with third and goal from the seven-yard line, hitting his tailback wide open in the left corner of the end zone. No extra point, Bryce stopping Mac on the one. It was 6–all. Then 12–12 at the half. The Bucs had gotten the lead, but then David had gone right at them, even though there were only ninety seconds left when the Stars got the ball back. It took four passes, two to Clay and two to Will, to get the Stars to the twelve. On first down, Clay lost the cornerback covering him on an outside move, cut the play over the middle—no fear—and then outfought Willie for the ball. David had thrown it high, almost like he was telling Clay, go get it, big boy. Clay did.

When the half ended twenty seconds later, Clay said to David, "I got him."

Meaning Willie.

"Won't be the last time" David said. He grinned. "You know what Coach calls a game like this, right?"

"Pure ball," Clay said.

By the middle of the fourth quarter, the Bucs were up a point, 19–18. The only thing that separated the two teams was a missed conversion by the Stars, David having just tripped over his own feet on a bootleg, even with nobody in front of him. But that trip, and that point, might've been enough to put the Bucs in first place alone if the Stars couldn't get one more score.

David was still hot when they got to the sideline. "We need somebody to make a play," he said. "I sure as heck didn't."

"Somebody will," Clay said. "This is our day. I can feel it."

David made a snorting sound.

Clay said, "I'm telling you, I get these feelings sometimes."

Maddie was with them. "He really does," she said.

"Usually only after he eats spicy food," David said.

"You have a very bad attitude sometimes, you know that, right?" Clay said to him.

"*You* just be right," David said.

Clay was. It just took longer than he would have liked—or preferred—for Bryce and the boys on defense to make him look like a prophet, at least to David. Because first he had to stand there and watch Mac Sherrill take the Bucs down the field, eating up yards and the clock, looking to slam the door on the Stars. Five minutes left. Four. Three. The Bucs finally found themselves on the Stars' thirty-four-yard line. Second and eight.

Mac hadn't just been keeping the ball on the ground. He'd made some safe throws, too, usually off sprint outs, still keeping the defense off balance, forcing them to respect his arm as much as his legs.

But on second down, he dropped straight back into the pocket for one of the first times the whole game, and the first time on this drive.

What he didn't count on was Jalen King coming from the outside on a corner blitz.

Jalen came from Mac's blind side, flying. Mac never saw him, never had a chance to get out of the way. Never even knew he was in trouble. He had just raised his arm, ready to cut the ball loose, when Jalen swatted at the ball, not taking a chance that Mac's arm would start forward. Ball dropped straight out of Mac's hand to his right, Jalen fell on it, Stars' ball, their own forty, minute and forty seconds left.

"You're welcome," Clay said to David.

"You didn't do anything," David said. "Jalen was the one."

"I was practically in his mind, like one of those Jedi mind things," Clay said. "Now let's go win the game."

David hit Clay on the right sideline for ten yards. Clay got out of bounds to stop the clock. Then David went to the left sideline, and hit Will. He got out of bounds. They were in Bucs' territory. No need yet to use a timeout. Josh ran up the middle for six yards. Then for six more. First down. Under a minute now.

David called his first timeout, one left after that, saying he wanted to give everybody a chance to catch their breath because the next breather any of them were going to get was when the Stars were in the end zone.

Maddie came out with water.

"Deep post," David said to Clay, "just in case you were wondering what the next play was. I didn't want to keep you in suspense."

"Thank you for that," Clay said. "And I love it."

When the ref blew his whistle to let them know the timeout was over, Maddie leaned close to Clay and said, "The corner blitz? That was all me."

"No way!" he said.

"Hush," she said. "But, yeah."

"He hadn't dropped back since the first quarter," Clay said.

She winked. "I get these feelings sometimes," she said.

The cornerback who'd been covering Clay for most of the game, Clay knew by now, was named Ted Wyatt. He was the same size as Clay, almost as fast. It had been a good battle between them from the start. Clay would help Ted up after a play, unless Ted helped him up first. When it was a good catch, Ted said so. Clay did the same after a good lick, or a deflection. Pure ball.

The last three passes Clay had caught had all been to the outside. David said that was why he'd called for the post; he felt like they had him set up perfectly for an inside move. "You do have a good inside move, right?" David had said as they broke the huddle.

"Almost positive," Clay said.

He made as good a head-and-shoulders fake to the outside as he had, at full speed. Ted bit. When he did, Clay got an inside shoulder on him, then was past him, running free in the middle of the field. Without seeing, he could feel Ted scrambling to catch up with him, knowing he couldn't, because the ball was already in the air.

Clay knew that Willie was up ahead of him somewhere, but he wasn't worrying about Willie then.

Just the ball.

Which David had underthrown, just a little.

Clay could see the ball was starting to knife toward the ground like a real good sinkerball in baseball. So at the last second, Clay went into a slide, both knees, getting as low as he could, wanting to get both arms underneath David's pass.

He did just as Ted Wyatt and Willie Sharpe—both of them more fixed on Clay than they were the ball, Ted coming from Clay's right and Willie from his left—went flying and crashing into each other.

Even as he was securing the ball, sure he'd kept it from hitting the ground, so low it felt as if he'd dug a hole for himself, he heard the sickening crash of their helmets.

When Clay wheeled around, he saw both of them stretched out on the ground.

All he could think of in that moment, seeing that neither one of them was moving, was this:

Could have been me.

Maybe *should* have been me.

Maybe that's why he jumped up the way he did and started screaming at them to get up.

# TWENTY-FOUR

*C*OME ON!" CLAY YELLED, AS if they were across the field from him, not lying at his feet. "Get up!"

He still had the ball under his arm. He could see the Bucs' coach running on the field. There was another man running alongside him. Players from both teams were there, too.

They were all staring at Ted and Willie. Nobody was saying anything.

Except Clay.

*"Why won't you get up?"*

His eyes were stinging as though he were holding back tears. He knew what he really wanted to tell them was to not be hurt, because they'd hit each other when they were trying to hit him.

But he could only say it to himself, taking his voice all the way down, not knowing if the words were even coming out of him, if they were still inside his head.

"Please don't be hurt," he said.

The ref closest to him came over, took the ball from him, gently said, "Why don't you just take a couple of steps back, son."

Clay felt a hand on his arm then, turned, and saw it belonged to David Guerrero.

"You gotta quiet down," he said to Clay. "People don't know whether to be looking at you or them."

"They need to be okay," Clay said.

"We all want that," David said. "But we gotta walk away."

"I must've crossed them up by dropping down low," Clay said.

"Everybody saw."

Clay said, "But I *heard*."

He and David stepped back, but only a yard or so. As they did, Clay saw Ted Wyatt give a little shake to his head as he started to roll himself up into a sitting position.

Then Willie did the same.

Clay felt as if he could breathe again.

He heard the man next to Willie say, "This is Dr. Reiner, Willie. Do you feel as if you ever lost consciousness?"

Willie slowly shook his head. "No, sir."

"Sure?"

Now Willie nodded.

"Yes, sir."

Then Willie looked at the doctor and said, "Ask you a question?"

"Sure."

"Did Eighty-Seven make the catch?"

Clay thought he saw the doctor smile.

"He did," the doctor said.

"Now *that* hurts, Doc," Willie said.

The coach helped Ted to his feet. Dr. Reiner helped Willie to his. The coach signaled toward the sideline, and two players came running in. One, Clay saw, was one of their wide receivers.

"You taking me out, Coach?" Willie said.

"Yes."

"*No!*" Willie Sharpe said.

Pure ball, Clay thought, even now, even after he'd gotten his bell rung like that.

"Doc can do a better job of checking you out on the sideline," the coach said.

"But there's still some game left," Willie said.

"But it's just a game, son," the coach said. "And there'll be other ones."

They switched now. The doctor walked with Ted Wyatt, holding on to his arm. The Bucs' coach put an arm around Willie's shoulders.

Without even thinking about what he was doing, Clay walked over to them.

"Can I do it?" he said to the coach.

The coach smiled. "Go ahead, Eighty-Seven."

Clay was the one putting his arm around Willie's shoulders now. He didn't say anything. Neither did Willie. They walked slowly toward the Bucs' bench, as if they were on the same team in that moment.

Maybe they were.

• • •

The Stars won the game three plays later. Clay made an inside fake this time, broke to the corner of the end zone behind Ted's replacement, caught a perfect lob throw from David, got both feet down inbounds. There were thirty seconds left. David's conversion pass was knocked down at the line, but it didn't matter. Stars 24, Bucs 19.

There was no big or loud or showy celebration when it was over. Oh, Clay and his teammates were happy. Just not as happy as they would have been without that collision at the end of deep post.

A collision that had thrown a different kind of scare into Clay Hollis.

About what could have happened.

He couldn't get the image of Ted and Willie lying on that field out of his mind. And every single time he thought about them— on the way home and into the night and when he was trying to fall asleep and couldn't—it wasn't the two of them Clay was seeing.

He was seeing himself.

# TWENTY-FIVE

**I**N THE CAR, CLAY SAID he didn't want to talk about the game, that he was just glad the Stars had won and that Willie and Ted were okay. His parents said okay. And they didn't talk about it at dinner, as quiet a dinner as Clay could remember, the sound of silverware on the plates sometimes the only noise at the kitchen table, where they were eating tonight.

When they were done, he said, "May I be excused?" His mom said, of course, she'd clean up. His dad asked if he'd be down to watch football later, and Clay said, maybe, but he was pretty tired. And went upstairs to his room. He had showered when he'd gotten home from the game, thinking that maybe if he scrubbed hard enough he could clean the memory of the two players on the field right off him. But he couldn't. He checked the messages on his phone, which he'd left upstairs during dinner, and saw one from Maddie:

Don't let this be a thing, either.

He didn't want it to be. But he couldn't help himself, the way he hadn't been able to help himself from yelling at them to get up. Nobody wanted to win more than he did. Just not like that. Nobody wanted to make a play more than he did when a game was on the line, but by making one today, he'd taken two players out of the game, and he knew it was just plain luck that neither one of them had gotten seriously injured. Somehow his mom, without Clay even seeing her do it, had talked to Willie's mom and Ted's mom after the game and gotten their phone numbers and asked them both to check in with her. They had. The only discussion at the dinner table that involved football had been when Katherine Hollis heard her phone buzz from the counter and saw the text message from Willie's mom that neither he nor Ted had suffered a concussion; both had been checked out right after the game.

To Clay, that felt like more of a win than winning the game.

But the bad feeling that wouldn't leave him was how easily it could have been him. How it could have been his helmet making the sickening sound he'd heard from Willie and Ted. How, in the words they always used about football, the words even Coach Coop used all the time, it could have been Clay's bell that got rung that way.

Clay knew it was early, knew there was football being played on television, but tonight he didn't care. He wanted to go to sleep, if he could, and hope that when he opened his eyes in the morning he wouldn't still be seeing Willie Sharpe and Ted Wyatt.

He had just turned off his lights when he saw his door open a crack, and saw his mom poke her head in.

"You okay?" she said.

"Just tired."

"You want to talk about it before you call it a night?"

"I acted like an idiot, Mom," he said, sitting up in his bed. "Yelling at them like that."

"You were concerned," she said. "You were scared for them. No crime there."

She came into his room and closed the door behind her and sat on the edge of his bed.

"I was scared for me," he said.

"I know, hon. I know."

"There's a lot going on," he said, thinking she didn't even know the half of it, because he'd never told her all he was carrying around in his head about Coach.

"At your age," she said, "there's always a lot going on. And a lot more good than bad, keep that in mind."

"I know," he said. "I know how lucky I am. It's just that every time somebody goes down now and doesn't get up right away, I always think it's something bad."

"But it wasn't today."

"Could have been."

"Clay," she said. "You think I don't hold my breath every time you get hit? I do. Your father laughs at me. Sometimes, as much as I love watching you and wanting you to do well, I close my eyes right before you get hit and don't open them again until he tells me you got up. But I've weighed the risks and rewards of you playing football. I've factored in the way you love it and the way I still love it, even though I know as much as I do about the risks."

"But you still let me play," Clay said.

"I let you play," she said. "So does your dad."

In the dark of his room, Clay said, "Ask you a question, Mom?"

"Anything."

"Do you still love football the way you always did?" he said.

She took a long time before answering. He could hear her sigh before she did.

"I don't," she said. "I still love it, don't get me wrong. I just love it a little less now."

"On a day like today," Clay said, "sometimes I feel the same way."

"In my heart," his mom said, "I still believe it's a great game. And it teaches you a lot. And shows people what kind of heart you have."

"I don't know as how I did that today," he said.

She got up then and kissed him on the top of his head.

"You weren't sitting where I was sitting," she said, "when you helped Willie Sharpe off that field."

Then she told him if he wanted to remember anything about today's game, to remember that. Told him to go to sleep. A few minutes later, he did.

Three games left.

Which meant it was simple now: Win out and they'd have the top seed going into the playoffs. The Stars would officially be the team to beat, if they weren't already.

The first of the three games was at home, Holy Cross field. The opponent was the Falcons, who'd lost as many games this season as they'd won. But if they won out and got a little luck with the teams ahead of them, they could make the Final Four, too. So there was no doubt that the Stars were going to see their very best game because they had even more on the line, knowing that one more loss would knock them out of the playoffs for sure. Clay's dad liked to quote a line from Bill Parcells, who, even though he was more famous for coaching the Giants and the Patriots into Super Bowls, had also coached the Cowboys once.

"When a game looks even," Coach Parcells had said, "bet the team that needs it more."

Clay reminded David and Bryce of that a couple of minutes before the kickoff.

"Hey," David said, "we always get the other guys' best game. So big whoop if it gets dialed up a little more today."

"Clay keeps talking about us being the team to beat," Bryce said. "That's why other teams try so hard to beat us."

From behind them, Maddie said, "Bryce, you really are a football genius."

"Yeah, and you're pretty funny for a girl."

"Or because I'm a girl," she said.

Bryce walked away, shaking his head. "You're always trying to trick me into saying something dumb."

Maddie called after him, "You really think that would require a trick?"

Bryce just waved his arm at her without looking back. "Funny, funny girl," they all heard him say.

What wasn't funny? The way the Stars played once the game started. Because once the game did start, they played their worst quarter of the season. By far.

Clay had dropped a sure touchdown pass the first time the Stars had the ball. Not because he was afraid of getting hit. Just because he flat dropped it. It was a fourth and goal from the Falcons' five. He had just put a killer move on Jack Stiles, a kid he knew from summer football camp, faking him to the inside, getting himself wide open outside, about three yards into the end zone. David put the ball right on his numbers, hard enough so that Jack didn't have a chance to recover, but not too hard to handle. And Clay just closed his arms too late and watched helplessly as the ball bounced off him and fell to the ground. The Falcons then went ninety-five yards on the Stars' defense, mostly keeping the ball on the ground, their O line opening up one huge hole after another, punishing the Stars' defense as much as any team had all season. Finally there was one more big hole and their tailback ran through it, untouched. They ran the exact same play on the conversion and it was 7–0.

While the two teams were lining up for the kick, Maddie came over and said, "I kept track in my head. You want to know how many plays that way?"

"A hundred?" Clay said.

"Twenty," she said. "I bet there hasn't been a twenty-play drive in our league all season. I think we might just have helped them make history."

"You know something?" Clay said. "Sometimes I don't love history nearly as much as you think."

The drive had eaten up so much clock that the first quarter was nearly over. Not just completely over. On the Stars' next drive, David suffered one of his few sacks since his concussion. Nobody'd put a body on the Falcons' right outside linebacker; he put a clean hit on David, right before his arm came forward. The ball dropped straight down behind him; the linebacker picked it up and ran thirty yards to the end zone. On the conversion, it looked as if Bryce was about to sack the Falcons' quarterback, Garrett Jones. Bryce was the one putting a hit on him, but somehow Garrett didn't go all the way down, stopped his fall with his left hand, got back up, and reversed his field. Now he was the one beating everybody into the end zone, and it was 14–0.

On the sideline, Clay said to David, "We've worked too hard to get to first place to give it up this easy."

"So let's start making things hard on those boys," David said. "They won the first quarter, we're gonna win the last three."

The Stars had one good, long drive in the second quarter. But again they ended up with a fourth down inside the ten. Again, Clay got loose from Jack Stiles. This time he didn't drop the ball. Just got separated from it when Jack came in from behind. Perfect timing. Big hit. Jack knocked the breath out of Clay at the same time he was hitting him hard enough to knock the ball loose. Game stayed 14–0. All Coach said to them right before the second half started was this:

"Now we got to play our best game in just half a game."

He went and stood by himself at midfield, the Stars' bench behind him. Clay saw Maddie come over and say something to him. Coach nodded. He smiled and patted her on her head, then went and got with the Stars' kicking team.

When the kicking team took the field, Coach waved Clay over to him.

"What's up, Coach?"

Coach said, "That girl over there, getting herself a drink of water? She sure knows her football."

"Boy, does she," Clay said.

"Who is she?" Coach said.

He actually sounded curious. Clay looked at him. He was smiling. But didn't seem to be kidding.

"I'm sorry," Clay said.

He had to be kidding. The only person from the team who spent more time with Coach than Clay was Maddie, now that she'd been doing her English project on Coach.

Just then, Clay heard the whistle from the field, meaning the second half was about to start, saw Marc Franklin setting the ball on his kicking tee, about to drive another one deep, just because he had one of the best legs in the league for doing that.

But Clay turned back to Coach, wanting some sign that he had just asked a serious question about Maddie, even if it had sounded that way.

"She's Maddie, Coach," he said. "Maddie Guerrero. You know her."

Coach Coop nodded. He was still smiling. "Not as well as she knows her football," he said. "She just told me we should try an onsides kick and, by God, that's what I told our kicker to do."

That's exactly what Marc Franklin did, spinning the ball to his right, the ball traveling ten yards the way it was supposed to, the way Marc had always worked on making it go ten yards in practice. Jalen King recovered. So there was no time for Clay to continue his conversation with Coach about Maddie; he was on his way back out to the field, a lot sooner than he'd expected, ready to play his own best game in the half game he had left.

He took one last look back at Coach, who shook a fist of encouragement at him. He was still smiling. Looking happy as could be.

Maybe he had just been joking. He'd try to figure that out later. All that mattered now, no joke, was figuring out a way to come from two scores down to beat the Falcons.

First down at the Stars' forty-five-yard line.

First things first.

The Stars scored after recovering the onsides kick. It was a good drive, the big play a crossing pattern over the middle to Clay after Josh had ripped off a good gain on a sweep. When they faced third and one from inside the Falcons' thirty, David made a call that was just all him, the football brain he already had, even in Pop Warner. He faked a handoff to Josh and threw the first deep ball he had all season to Marc Franklin, his tight end.

The fake to Josh set everything up. He crouched over as if he had the ball, went right through the line, got tackled by the Falcons' middle linebacker. The free safety had pinched up, too, before he realized that David was the one with the ball and was throwing it to Marc, who didn't have a defender anywhere near him. It was 14–6. They were finally on the board. David threw it to Will for the extra point and it was 14–7.

When Clay came off the field, he walked right over to Maddie. "Onsides kick?"

"I never thought Coach would go for it," she said. "But he did!"

"He say anything to you after?"

"Yeah," she said. "Something about how I sure know my football. Why?"

"Just wondering," Clay said, and bumped her some fist.

The game stayed at 14–7 until the last minute of the third quarter when Bryce jumped a screen pass perfectly, stepped in front of the Falcons' tailback, and ran half the field for a touchdown. They were set to tie the game, except Jack Stiles somehow got a hand on the ball at the last second to slap away David's pass to Clay for the conversion. So they were down a point. But there was still a quarter to play, as if the game had turned their way. Or the great half game that Coach had told them they were going to play.

The Falcons got off another good drive, but then their quarterback, Garrett Jones, shocked everybody including himself by dropping a snap on a fourth and one from the Stars' fifteen. Then the Stars were the ones grinding out a drive, eating up the clock, keeping the ball on the ground for a change because Josh was getting four or five yards every time he touched the ball. They were past midfield, on the Falcons' forty, third and eight, when David said he was ready to air it out and called for the same play that had caused Willie Sharpe and Ted Wyatt to collide in the Bucs game, not just collide but end up down—and so Clay thought at the time—and out.

This time David's pass wasn't short or low. If anything, it looked like it might be a little high. Clay had Jack Stiles beaten, two good steps on him, and was fixed on the ball now, wondering whether he might have to leap for it, when he took his eye off it for just a moment because he saw the Falcons' strong safety coming for him, full tilt, the way Willie Sharpe had.

And Clay stopped.

Stopped and watched as the ball went over his head and into the hands of the free safety backing up the play, like he was a center fielder in baseball who'd been positioned perfectly. And felt like the crash this time was his heart hitting the pit of his stomach.

# TWENTY-SIX

**A**T LEAST CLAY HAD ENOUGH player in him to chase the kid down and shove him out of bounds in front of the Falcons' bench before he could turn the play upfield.

The run back to his own bench felt like the longest he'd ever taken in football. Somehow he could feel Coach Coop's eyes on him the whole play. They were still on Clay when he got to the Stars' bench. Coach wasn't smiling now. Just looking extremely alert.

He waved Clay over to him, same as he had when he'd told Clay about the onsides kick, right before he'd asked who Maddie was.

"I'd ask what happened, son," Coach said. "But I saw what happened. And you-all know what did."

Clay could hear, could *feel*, the game going on behind him. But his whole focus was on Coach. The way Coach was focused on him.

"At the very last second," Clay said, "I remembered what happened in the last game."

"Probably wish you could've forgotten that part," Coach said, "those two boys crashing into each other the way they did." Coach clapped his hands together. In that moment, the sound was like a thunderclap to Clay. "Something like that," Coach said.

Clay looked down. "Yeah," he said. "Like that."

In a soft voice Coach said, "Look at me when I'm talking to you, son."

Clay did.

Coach said, "So you pulled up, like you done before this season."

"Yes, sir."

"Thought we'd already moved past that."

"Me too."

"Only it turns out we didn't."

"Not on that play. No, sir."

Clay heard a cheer come up from the Stars' bench. He turned quickly, saw that Bryce had just sacked Garrett Jones for a big loss. Then Clay turned back to Coach and said, "I'm so sorry."

"Not looking for an apology. Just trying to figure out what we got to do to get past this again."

Clay thought about something his dad had told him once, about how the truth wasn't supposed to be a last resort, but a first.

"I didn't want to get hit in the head," Clay said.

The next part came out of him before he could do anything about that.

"I've learned so much stuff this season about what can happen if you get hit too hard in the head," Clay said. "I don't want to end up . . ."

He stopped himself there. Too late. He saw it on Coach's face before Coach even opened his mouth.

"You mean you don't want to ever end up like me," Coach Coop said.

"I didn't mean it that way."

"Sure you did," Coach said. "Course you did."

Then he put a hand on Clay's shoulder. "You can play this game a lot smarter than I ever did, partly because of what you've studied up on," he said. "But what you can't do is play it like you just did. Or you got to find yourself another game."

Another cheer from the Stars' bench. Clay couldn't help it— he checked the field again, saw the Stars' punt return team heading out there, knowing they were about to get the ball back.

Coach's hand was still on Clay's shoulder pad. "I told you boys the first day we were together that I'd never ask you to do something you can't. And I never will. Told you I'd never ask you to *be* something you're not."

He crouched down in front of Clay on those bad knees. Clay could see the pain on his face just doing that. But now they were eye to eye.

"Gonna ask you something straight up," Coach said. "Are you a football player or not?"

"I am," Clay said.

"Then get back out there and show me," Coach Coop said.

Clay watched Jalen King make a fair catch on the punt. Clay ran toward the huddle and toward his teammates, feeling like he already had the ball under his arm, like he wanted to take it to the house.

The Stars started out on their thirty-three-yard line, three minutes left, down a point. They either stayed in first place, or dropped down. It wasn't the end of the world if they did that, if they did drop down in the standings, everybody on the Stars knew that. But to Clay, this was about more than just the record now. This was about pride. In his whole life, since the time he'd started playing organized football, he had never wanted to make a play, to help win his team a game, more than he did right now. He wanted to make a play and be a player. Coach had just called him out on that. He'd done it in a nice way. But what he'd really done is ask him who he was.

*So who are you?*

Was he the guy who'd overcome his fears before and gone on to make every tough catch he was asked to make in traffic? Or was he the guy who'd acted more afraid of getting hit than he was of the dark when he was little?

Sometime before the end of this game, he was going to find out.

Before they all got in the huddle, David grabbed Clay by the arm and walked him a few yards away.

"Gotta ask, dude?" David said. "Is there any play I can't call?"

It stung, hearing his best friend put it to him like that. But Clay knew he had a right to ask. He wanted the game, too.

"You can throw the whole playbook at them," Clay said. "But first chance you get, throw me the ball."

They got a first down, keeping the ball on the ground. Then David threw a quick curl to Marc. On second down, he called Clay's number, a quick slant, but to the outside. Clay bobbled the ball, but managed to have it under control before he ran out of bounds. First down. Clock stopped. Under two minutes. Two timeouts left. It was like they had all day.

David wanted to go to Clay again, again on an outside cut, but Jack Stiles had him covered the whole way, and David had to throw the ball away. David threw it to Will on the other side of the field then, for eight yards. Third and two.

In the huddle, David looked right at Clay. "Ball fake, post," he said. It meant he was going to fake the ball to Josh, with the Falcons expecting them to run a short-yardage play, and then look for Clay.

Over the middle. Middle of the defensive secondary.

"Okay," Clay said.

David snorted. "I don't call plays if I don't think they're okay," he said.

Clay ran out to his position on the right side. He could feel his heart beating like he'd just run the whole length of the field. His mouth was so dry he could barely swallow. By now he knew that football could find all sorts of ways to test you. And how the game had a way of finding you.

It was about to do that now.

And ask him to stick his head in there.

Jack Stiles was expecting another outside move, after two of those in a row. Clay gave him a quick head fake and then beat him to the inside easily, creating separation right away. When he finally looked back for the ball, it was already in the air. So this was like all the other times in their lives when David had trusted Clay enough to throw the ball on his break.

"Need help!" Jack Stiles yelled from behind him, as Clay realized, tracking the ball, that David had led him by a little too much.

Truth or dare.

You had to want it, Coach said.

Clay laid out for the ball, arms out in front of him as far as they would go, almost like he was diving without leaving his feet.

Only worried about making the catch, not about what might be coming from the other direction.

But defenseless.

He felt the ball on his fingertips, then in his hands, then in his arms. Somebody, probably one of the safeties—he wasn't checking numbers at that point—hit him one second later, spinning him around, back in the direction the ball had just come. But when he landed on his left side, the ball was secure, he had both arms underneath it. He knew it was a good catch.

No.

A *great* catch.

He felt some pain where he'd landed on his left shoulder. Didn't care. All he cared about was that he made the catch and taken the hit.

Player, he thought.

*Player.*

Four plays later, David snuck in from the half-yard line. He threw an inside slant to Clay for the conversion. Stars 20, Falcons 14, final.

# TWENTY-SEVEN

O N THE CAR RIDE HOME Clay's mom and dad kept telling him how proud they were that he'd come back the way he had after what had happened on the interception.

"I just did what I should've done in the first place," he said.

His mom said, "You found a way to face down your fears." She turned around from the front seat and smiled. "Mine, too."

"What your mom is trying to say is that we're allowed to be proud of you," Ben Hollis said. "And you earned that game ball even if you wouldn't take it."

Coach had tried to give Clay the game ball. But as soon as he handed it to him, Clay handed it right over to Bryce Darrell, telling him that nothing at the end would have mattered if he hadn't turned the game around with his pick six.

Clay put his head back on the backseat now and felt himself smiling. He had picked up a lot of information this season, and his mom had picked up a lot more, just being Mom. But today the information had been about him. The stuff he'd found out, that was about *him*. He felt like he'd won as much of a victory over himself as the Stars had over the Falcons.

Pretty good day, all in all.

Pretty *great* day.

Like that catch.

The Stars finally finished with the top seed in the league. Playoffs were scheduled to start next Saturday, Stars against the Vikings, the only team to have beaten them all season, way back in September, almost as if that game had happened in a season other than the one they were playing.

By now, Maddie had finished her paper on Coach and her video and gotten a total screaming A. She'd done all of her interviews with Coach on Saturdays after the last three games of the regular season. Clay had always gone with her to Coach's apartment. Sometimes—a lot of times, actually—when Coach couldn't find the answer to the question Maddie had asked him, she'd hit the pause button, and Clay would fill in the gap because of all the research of Monty Cooper's career he'd done himself. And then they'd just keep going.

The best part of the video, or so Clay thought, was the part at the end when Maddie just trained her camera on Coach's scrapbooks, Clay slowly turning the pages.

Clay tried not to think about how those scrapbooks might be the only memories Coach'd have someday. Or who was going to take care of Coach down the road. He knew that someday, maybe someday soon, he would have to talk to his parents about that.

Just not until the season was over, and ending the way Clay wanted it to, the Stars winning two more games and a championship and Coach getting to AT&T Stadium on Thanksgiving Day.

Over the past few weeks Clay hadn't noticed any big change in Coach. If his memory wasn't getting any better, it didn't seem to be getting any worse. He watched him closely. Maddie watched even more closely, like a hawk.

He had gotten lost just one more time that they knew about, the week before their last regular-season game. Coach was supposed to be on his way home after a doctor's appointment—the doctor wanted to clean out Coach's right knee one more time, Coach was fighting him on that—and ended up at Holy Cross field instead of back at his apartment.

He had known enough to call Clay, asking him wherever everybody was, practice was about to start.

"Hold on a second," Clay said.

He was in the kitchen, helping his mom set up for dinner when he'd seen COACH on his phone. He pressed the phone to his chest and said, "This is about football, gotta take it," and headed upstairs to his room, shutting the door behind him.

"Sorry," he said to Coach. "You're at the field?"

"Where is everybody?" Coach said.

"There's no practice tonight, Coach," he said.

There was a long silence at Coach's end, before he finally said, "What do you mean? Of course there's practice!"

Clay remembered the lost look in Coach's eyes the night they picked him up at the police station. "Coach . . . are you okay?"

For a second Coach didn't say anything. Then he sighed

and said, "I just want to go home," in a voice Clay would barely hear.

"And we're gonna get you home," Clay said. "No worries."

In the same low voice, Coach said, "Speak for yourself, son."

Clay reminded Coach how to put his phone on speaker. It took some doing, even for that. At one point Clay heard the phone drop and heard Coach curse. But when he had it back in his hand and on speaker, Clay told him to go to Waze and hit the button in the lower-left-hand corner of the screen, and hit HOME.

Coach did that.

"There she goes," he said. "It says I'm twenty minutes away."

"You are," Clay said. "Just listen to Rita the rest of the way."

He'd taken to calling the woman's voice on Waze "Rita."

"She'll get you home," Clay said. "We got this."

"I'd been doing so good," Coach said.

It was hard to tell whether he was talking to Clay, or to himself.

"You've been doing awesome, Coach," Clay said. "Just got dropped for a loss this one time."

"Okay."

"Call me when you're home," Clay said, knowing that he was going to track Coach all the way back to his apartment, anyway.

"Sorry to bother you," Coach Coop said.

"You never bother me," Clay said.

"I'll be fine now," Coach said.

Then he told Clay that there was an old country line that covered this.

"If the phone don't ring," he said, "you'll know it's me."

Said this wouldn't happen again.

But it did.

Coach had scheduled an extra practice this week, and the league allowed it, saying that as long as the Stars didn't have any contact drills, didn't scrimmage, they could get together on Tuesday and Wednesday and Thursday nights. The extra practice was on Thursday. Coach said he wanted them all to be together, whether it looked like flag football or not.

"Now you-all know, same as I do, that these aren't gonna be our last practices this season," he said on Tuesday night. "But because this *is* football, and that ball *will* bounce funny on you, there is a chance that they could be. So what I want us to do, and without sounding like I've gone soft as gravy on you, is to just appreciate being together as a team as much as we can."

He had looked around at all of them, turning one way and then the other and said, "Trust me on something: Even more than the wins and losses, what you remember best is that you shared something."

He swallowed and said, "And there isn't nobody who can ever take that away from you, because it will be in your hearts forever."

Now it was a quarter to six on Thursday night, practice scheduled to start at six. Clay and David and most of their teammates had been there since five. Nobody had told them to show up that early. They just had, maybe because they had taken Coach's message from the other night into their own hearts, and planned to make every moment they had together count.

But Coach wasn't there.

Maddie pulled Clay aside and said, "He should be here by now."

"I know."

"You check your phone?"

Maddie nodded, her face looking grim. "He did what he's not supposed to do, and turned it off. Or it's run out of power."

"Great."

"Let me look again," she said, whipped her phone out of her back pocket. "He's turned it back on!"

"So where is he?"

Maddie was frowning, looking at the phone and then at Clay. "Olmos Park."

"Why?"

"Gee, I don't know, why don't I ask him?"

She jabbed a finger at the phone. "Straight to voice mail," she said.

"Olmos Park is where Coach and I ended up the first night he got lost," Clay said.

Then: "Try calling him again."

Maddie did. And shook her head.

"What do we do now?" she said.

"We go get him," Clay said.

# TWENTY-EIGHT

**M**ADDIE GRINNED AT CLAY. SHE was worried about Coach; they were both worried about Coach. But this still felt like the beginning of an adventure.

"Your parents' Uber account or mine?" she said.

"Go for it," Clay said. "We'll figure out a way to explain it to them later."

"Is this okay, what we're doing without telling anybody?" she said.

"Making sure *Coach* is okay is all that matters," he said.

While Maddie did what she had to do on her phone to call for an Uber car, Clay ran over to David and said, "You start walking the guys through plays when they're all here. Heck, you call them in games, might as well do it in practice."

"Where are you going?"

Clay said, "Coach is having some trouble getting to practice. Maddie and I are going to get him."

Before David could ask another question, Clay said, "Be back in a few."

He and Maddie ran for the parking lot. She said the car was only five minutes away. Clay asked if she'd ever used her parents' account before and she said no, but they'd showed her how to use it, in case she ever needed it.

"And now you do," Clay said.

"Yeah," she said. "Now I do."

The driver was a nice woman who said her name was Pam. She asked them if their parents would be okay with this. Clay and Maddie said they would, it was kind of an emergency, then told her they were going to Olmos Park.

"Emergency as in somebody being sick?" Pam said.

"As in, somebody just needing us to go pick him up," Clay said.

In a lot of ways, he thought.

On the way to Olmos Park, Maddie kept checking to make sure Coach hadn't moved. He hadn't. She kept trying to call him. His phone kept sending her straight to voice mail. The only good news, if there was any, was that he hadn't turned off his phone again. And it still had power.

"Maybe he just forgot we had practice," Clay said. "We've practiced twice a week all season. He didn't even schedule this one until a couple of days ago, so it wasn't on your weekly calendar for him."

"Yeah," Maddie said, not much enthusiasm in her voice. "Maybe."

"C'mon," Clay said, "that could be it."

Maddie said, "Fingers crossed."

They stopped talking then. When they got to the park, Clay asked Pam if she could hang around for just a couple of minutes. She turned and smiled at them and said, "I kind of get what's happening here. Whatever you two need."

They both thanked her.

"You are," she said, "more than welcome."

He was on the same bench where he'd sat with Clay that night. His legs were stretched out in front of them, because he said stretching them out that way would help with the pain sometimes. Clay could see he was wearing the faded Cowboys cap he'd wear to practice sometimes, the one with the lone star on it.

"Hey, Coach," Clay said.

Coach turned and looked at him, tilting his head a little to the side, almost like he was trying to place the face. "Hey, hoss," he said.

He nodded at Maddie. "See you brought your friend," he said. "One with all those x's and o's inside her pretty head."

"Yes," Maddie said, "he did."

She sat on one side of Coach, Clay on the other.

"What's going on?" Clay said.

Coach looked at him, smiled, and shrugged.

"We came here one time, didn't we?"

"We did," Clay said. "Had a real good talk that night."

"Thought so."

"So how'd you happen to end up here?" Maddie said.

Coach shrugged again. "Just drove."

He didn't seem upset or confused. Just lost. Again.

"Well, as nice as it is here," Clay said, "we got to get you to practice now. Last one before the big game."

"When's practice?" Coach said.

"Now," Maddie said. "And we're not having it without you."

He focused his attention on Maddie now. Smiling again. "Must've forgot," he said. "Happens to me more and more."

"Everybody forgets stuff," Clay said.

"Not like me."

He sat there, as if in no rush to leave. The scene in front of them wasn't so different from the last time Clay had been here with him. A little girl in glasses on the slide, her mom waiting for her at the bottom. A man throwing a Frisbee and his dog chasing it. A boy and girl walking away from them, holding hands.

"Coach isn't supposed to forget when there's practice," Coach said. "Sort of become my thing lately."

Maddie said, "It's my fault. I should have told you to put it on your to-do list."

If he heard her, he didn't act as if he did. "So we're going to practice now?"

"Yup," Clay said. "You're gonna drive me and Maddie there."

"You know where to go?"

Maddie said they sure did. Then she ran to tell Pam, the driver, that she could leave. When she got back, she and Clay and Coach walked toward his truck. None of them spoke until they were all inside, and Maddie was checking her own Waze and telling Coach to take a right as they came out of Olmos Park.

Maddie muted the woman's voice on her phone. She told Coach when to take a right or left, and he would just nod and do it. It wasn't until they got to Holy Cross that he spoke to them again.

"I just forgot," he said.

# TWENTY-NINE

I T WAS THE SATURDAY MORNING of the Stars-Vikings
game, the one that would put the winner into the championship game in a week. The kick was scheduled for one o'clock.
The Stars were supposed to show up an hour before that at Holy
Cross field.

Clay was already in his uniform by eleven, alone in his room.

All football Saturday mornings were special to him; he knew
that by now. You only got so many of them every year. Sometimes
Clay wondered how he could ever be more excited than he felt
right now when he graduated to the world of Friday Night Lights
in Texas high school football, if he was good enough and lucky
enough to do that.

This wasn't just game day. This was more. This was *big* game
day, for him and for his teammates. And even for Coach, even
though he played bigger games than this in his own life, times
a thousand.

Just thinking about Coach made Clay reach down for his phone, there next to him at the end of his bed, and go straight to Find My Friends. When he did, he saw that Coach was already at the field. So maybe they were the same today. Maybe, after all the football Coach had had in his life, he still couldn't wait to get to the field.

Maybe, Clay thought, Coach didn't need any kind of GPS this morning, didn't need any kind of help from his own phone to find his way to the big game.

Clay's mom opened his bedroom door, saw him sitting there, with everything except his helmet on, and smiled.

"Please tell me you didn't sleep that way," she said.

"Thought about it, not gonna lie," he said. "Everything except my shoulder pads."

"So I take it you're ready to get after it, and we should move up our time of departure?"

She was smiling at him. He smiled back. "Pretty much."

"Been some ride, hasn't it?" she said. "With a few bumps in the road, of course."

"And ending up in a few ditches," Clay said.

She came over and sat down next to him. "It's a hard-knocks game," she said, "even when you're twelve. And that never changes. I saw it with your uncles and now I'm seeing it with you."

"Tell me about it," Clay said.

She turned so she was facing him and picked up his right hand and squeezed it with both of her own. "You know I haven't been trying to scare you away from football, right?" she said. "Because sometimes I think some of my information overload might have done that."

"I would have found out that stuff on my own," Clay said. "Heck, you know I *have* found out a lot of stuff on my own."

He didn't tell her that so much of what he'd read and learned hadn't been as much about what football might do to him as what it had already done to Coach.

"I just want to tell you again, big boy, that if I honestly thought football was too dangerous for you to play, I wouldn't let you keep playing. Someday you'll be old enough to make that choice yourself. But for now, it's still mine and your dad's."

"I know that."

She said, "What I honestly do believe is that the things football has taught you just this season . . ." She gave his hand a squeeze. "It's like they say in Texas: It ain't nothin'."

"No, it's not."

His mom stood up.

"Are you thinking what I'm thinking?" she said. "Because what I'm thinking is that we might as well head on over there right now."

"You really are a mind reader sometimes."

Clay stood up, went over, and picked up his helmet off his desk, thinking that the only thing that scared him about football today was that he might have run out of Saturdays.

To Clay, Coach seemed like his old self today, the Coach Coop he'd met at the very start of the season, before he started forgetting things and getting lost. And trying to hide his own fears about that as best as he could.

While the Stars stretched on the field, Coach walked among them, occasionally stopping to say something to one of his players.

It was something he hadn't done since the first few games of the season. Maybe it was a way of showing them and showing himself that he was the same guy he had always been, even though Clay knew better.

When he'd made his way over to Clay, Coach said, "Not expecting too much from you today, Eighty-Seven. Well, other than you playing a scrapbook game of your own."

Five minutes before the kickoff, he gathered the Stars in a circle around him and pretty much told the rest of them the same thing he'd told Clay.

"When you're young, like you-all are," he said, "you think you're gonna have as many days like this as you could ever want. And guess what? Some of you might be as lucky as I was and get 'em, in high school and college and maybe even in the National Football League."

Same deal as always, Clay thought. Coach always made "National Football League" sound like some kind of church.

"Some of you," Coach continued, "might turn out to be what I like to call one of the fortunate few."

He paused then. And didn't pick up his train of thought right away. Clay was worried that this might be another way for him to get lost.

But he wasn't.

"I'm not the best one with words, you boys know that by now," he said. "But I want you to know that the only Saturday that matters is the one we got right here in front of us, like a present we're about to unwrap."

He smiled.

"So let's go do that," he said. "Let's go find out what's inside."

They came in, tightening the circle, and yelled, "Go Stars!" When Clay walked away, Maddie was with him.

"He seems good today," she said.

"It's all good," Clay said.

David came over. "Let's go have a game of catch," he said. "To get us ready for the big game."

"Yup," Clay said. "I'll get open and you get it to me."

"Best game plan we ever had," David Guerrero said.

He put up his right hand for a high five. Clay slapped his hand, hard. Maddie went over and stood next to Coach. Clay saw Coach pat her on the head. They both looked happy. It's was like Coach always said: Where else in the world would you want to be if a game was about to break out?

This time a beauty broke out.

The Stars scored first, David crossing up the Vikings by calling for a reverse to Clay from the Vikings' eight, Clay coming around behind David from the right, taking a pitch, getting around the corner, having just enough room to dive for the pylon and get there when Tayshawn Moore, the Vikings' middle linebacker, looked like he still might have an angle on him.

"Great dive," David said, jerking Clay to his feet.

"Great *call*," Clay said. "Is that what you meant by a game of catch?"

"Just with an extremely short toss," David said.

Josh ran it in for the conversion, David pitching it to him this time and even acting as a blocker. It was 7–0. But then the Vikings shut down pretty much everything the Stars tried on offense for the rest of the half while the Stars' D was doing the same to the Vikings' offense. It looked like the Stars might take that 7–0 lead into halftime, but with a minute left, Jalen King fell down like he was tripping over the thirty-yard stripe; Luke Byrnes threw it to Michael Moretti, his fastest wideout. It was 7–6. Luke kept it himself for the point. Game tied.

"I can't believe I fell down like that!" Jalen said when they were all off the field.

"Anybody can do that," Clay said. "Now you just got to show the guys over on the other side how you get back up."

The Stars tried to take back control of the game with their first drive of the third quarter. David, still calling his own game, did that by coming out throwing. By the time they had a first down at the Vikings' thirteen, Clay was pretty sure David had at least one completion on the drive to every receiver he had. The big play was to Clay, a slant to the outside that he turned into a long gainer when he got away from Henry Morales, the kid covering him, with a pretty sweet straight-arm.

Now David tried to go back to Clay for the score. He sent him on a cross, over the middle, back of the end zone. Clay beat Henry clean. But Tayshawn had dropped back into coverage, David never saw him, threw the ball right to him. Tayshawn dropped to the ground with him, not even trying to run the ball out, too many Stars around. Touchback. Vikings' ball, out to the twenty.

Even when the play was over, David hadn't moved from the spot from which he'd thrown the ball, staring at where Tayshawn had been, like he couldn't believe his eyes, as if Tayshawn had appeared out of nowhere.

Clay went over to him. "C'mon," he said. "Let's get out of here. We'll get it back."

"That's the worst throw I've made all season," David said. "And the total worst possible time."

"Lot of game left," Clay said, now pulling him toward the Stars' bench.

"How did I not see him?"

"Happens."

"Not to me, it doesn't."

"Our D will stop them," Clay said. "And then you'll take us down the field again."

Only their D *didn't* stop them. Luke Byrnes took *his* team down the field, eighty yards, using up so much clock that he took the game out of the third quarter and into the fourth, running it himself more than throwing it, finally giving it to his tailback, Joey Foss, three straight times from inside the Vikings' ten until Joey scored. It was 13–7. And it looked like it was about to be 14–7 until Bryce Darrell somehow fought off two blockers and stuck up a hand and knocked away the conversion pass that Luke had intended for Michael Moretti.

So they were down six. They made a couple of first downs, but the Vikings stopped them, and forced a punt. But then the Stars' defense forced a punt, holding the Vikings at midfield. Stars' ball at their twenty-five. Four minutes, five seconds left. They were seventy-five yards from a score and a conversion that would put them in the title game.

Or there was that much time left in their season. Not much riding on this next series, not much at all, Clay thought.

"I can't make any more mistakes," David said to Clay.

"Mistakes?" Clay said. "What the heck are you talking about? What you're about to make are plays."

They weren't big plays. Just a lot of small ones, that just kept adding up. Five-yard run from Josh. Short pass to Clay on the outside. Same to Will Kellerman on the other side. Move the chains. Work the clock. Everybody knew they weren't going to get the ball back if they didn't score now, at least not this season.

They were at the Vikings' thirty with two minutes left. Josh ran it twice. Then David threw a screen to him. He got four yards and a first down, inside the twenty. The Vikings called their last timeout, just to give their guys a breather. The Stars weren't the only ones playing for their season.

David stayed conservative. Another handoff to Josh for five yards. Then he straightened out, threw it to Clay before Clay even moved off the line. Another first down.

Under a minute.

David didn't call the Stars' last timeout there. Coach did. Clay looked over, saw him say something to Maddie before she ran out on the field with her water bottles.

And a play, as it turned out.

She said to her brother, "Coach wants you to run Eighty-Seven post."

David shook his head. "No, he doesn't."

"Yeah," Maddie said, "he sort of does."

They all knew it was the same play David had called when

Tayshawn picked him off in the end zone. And David hadn't gone back over the middle since.

Like he was the one afraid to go over the middle now.

Maddie left. David watched her go. He looked over at Coach. Who nodded at him and then turned his back and walked a few yards down the sideline from where he'd been standing.

David shook his head, stepped back inside the huddle, knelt down, told the rest of the guys the play. As they broke the huddle, Clay gently grabbed David's face mask and said, "Game . . . of . . . catch."

Then Clay said, "Got it?"

"Got it."

"*I'll* get it," Clay said.

Clay ran out to his spot. Henry Morales was as close to him as he could be without being offsides. Letting Clay know he was going to be crowding him right off the snap.

Clay was the one who nearly jumped offsides, nearly jumped the count, wanting to get a step on Henry. But he didn't jump the count, didn't even make an outside move, just got a quick step inside on Henry, using strength as well as speed to muscle past him, get clear of him, and run for the goalposts again. Back of the end zone. Again.

David never hesitated, threw what Coach liked to call a pea, right on Clay's numbers. Clay held on to the ball as if for dear life. It was 13–all.

No celebration after he made the catch.

Just hand the ball to the ref.

Still work to be done.

It was short work. David dropped back, looked to his right, as if he were going back to Clay, even pump-faked in his direction. Then looked to his left and lobbed the ball to the left corner of the end zone to Josh Bodeen, who'd snuck out of the backfield and gotten back there, wide-open. Josh would say that he felt like it took forever for the ball to get to him. When it did, he smothered it with his arms. Then he just sat down, looking as if he just might sit there with it forever.

Stars 14, Vikings 13.

Game over. Just not their season.

The Vikings had time for two plays after the kickoff, Luke trying to throw the ball as far as he could both times. The last throw, to Michael Moretti down the sidelines, was so far out of bounds that Maddie made her first catch of the season.

Coach turned to David then.

"Can't play this game afraid," he said.

# THIRTY

**B**Y THE TIME CLAY GOT home, he'd learned on social media that the Bucs had won their semifinal game. So the Stars and Bucs would do it again, not so long after Clay thought their two teams had played the game of the year in San Antonio Pop Warner, at least until Willie Sharpe and Ted Wyatt had run into each other. Clay's mom always told him that sports was in the memory-making business.

Just not a memory like Willie and Ted laid out on the field the way they had been.

But Clay told himself that he could wait until tomorrow to start to get fixed on next Saturday, told himself to enjoy the game they'd just played against the Vikings, and the way they'd won it, with David being the one to overcome his fears this time. Clay had been thinking about it since the game ended:

When that ball had been in the air at the very end, he hadn't spent one second worrying about what might happen to him, what kind of hit he might take if he was able to make the catch. He was more worried about David making his throw.

Man, he thought, he'd traveled a long way to make that catch.

After dinner Clay FaceTimed with David for a long while, as they replayed nearly everything that had happened against the Vikes, all the way through their last drive against them. And then they talked a little bit about the Bucs, they couldn't help it, how they'd both learned from Facebook and Insta that Willie Sharpe had even scored one of his team's touchdowns today on a punt return. Clay told David he actually felt happy to find that out, find out that Willie wasn't just back playing, he was playing at his best. By now, Clay had learned that Willie's parents had made him sit out one game after his collision with Ted, same as Ted's had, just as a precaution, even though neither one of them had been diagnosed with a concussion.

"I want everybody at their best next week," Clay said to David. He saw David nod.

"Same," David said.

Right before Clay went to bed, he remembered to send Maddie a text.

Alamo tomorrow?

The reply seemed to come about five seconds later.

Took u long enuf, loser.

In the late morning they walked along Alamo Street, which ran next to Alamo Plaza, knowing by now, after all the trips the two of them had made here, that they were in the general area where the south wall had been in 1836, and where the main gate had been. And knew that it was on the east side of the main gate where Colonel James Bowie had died.

Clay and Maddie had talked about even paying fifteen dollars each today and doing something neither one of them had done in a while: take the official Battlefield Tour. But even though they'd brought money, they decided against it after Clay's mom dropped them off.

"I like our unofficial tour better," Maddie said.

"Totally," Clay said. "Heck, you could probably be a better guide than the real guides."

"You're not so bad yourself, Eighty-Seven," she said.

So they just did their favorite thing and wandered. Happy to be here and happy to be here together, though Clay would never say that to Maddie. They went through the Long Barrack, taking their time, and then went and found some shade behind the Alamo Church, which they knew had been rebuilt the first time after the original battle in '36.

Sometimes they'd go five minutes, or more, without saying anything, not because they didn't have anything to say, just because sometimes the thing that they both remembered, truly, about the Alamo, was a reverence for the ones who had fought and died here that seemed to ask for quiet, or even demand it.

Eventually they ended up near the big lawn in the courtyard, noticing a lot of brown in it today, making it like most lawns in San Antonio after the fall had turned out to be as dry as the summer had been. They sat down on one of the courtyard benches.

"You ever notice," Maddie said, "how we never go into the gift shop and buy anything when we come here?"

"The things I like the best about the Alamo aren't for sale," he said.

"You mean the history?"

Clay laughed. "Hey, it's not like they're not selling a whole bunch of history in that gift shop."

"Our gifts are way better," Maddie said. Her smile stretched wide.

"I just hope we did the right thing."

"We always do," said Maddie.

They finally got around to talking about yesterday's game then, about Coach sending in the first play he'd sent in to David in a while.

"He even called me by name before he did!" Maddie said. "Something else he hadn't done in a while."

"I just think he has good days and bad days," Clay said. "And yesterday was a good one. Or a good 'un, as he'd say."

"A real good 'un," Maddie said. "Before he told me what play he wanted to run, he said, 'If your brother goes to the outside one more time with Eighty-Seven, he's gonna get picked, 'cause the cornerback's sitting on it.'"

"It means he still sees a lot more than we think."

"Sometimes," Maddie said.

There was another long silence between them until Clay said, "When the season's over, we have to say something."

"To our parents, you mean."

"Yeah. We're not going to be able to keep track of him when he doesn't have football."

"What *is* he gonna have when he doesn't have football?" she said.

"Us," Clay said.

"Seriously, though. What else?"

"He's gonna have us," Clay said again.

Before Clay texted his mom and asked her to come get them, they took one more walk past the Wall of History, talked about all the men who had made "Remember the Alamo" as famous a rallying cry as there had ever been in Texas, or anywhere else.

"I wonder sometimes if they thought they were being brave," Clay said. "Or if they were just too busy doing what they thought soldiers were *supposed* to do."

"Probably a little bit of both."

"But they kept fighting even when they knew they had no chance," Clay said. "That they were losing with no chance of winning."

"Guess that's why we're still talking about them, what, a hundred and eighty years later?" Maddie said. "My history teacher was talking about the Alamo the other day, and said what it really proves is that courage lasts forever."

Clay texted his mom then, and they started walking toward the front entrance.

"Think about it," Maddie said. "How do you keep fighting even when you know what the ending is going to be?"

"Coach does," Clay said.

# THIRTY-ONE

**C**LAY'S MOM AND DAD INVITED Coach Coop over for dinner the night before the championship game.

They'd originally planned to ask him over the next night, after the Bucs game. But Coach told Clay's mom that if somehow—wasn't going to happen, not in this world—but *somehow* the Stars lost the game, it wouldn't be much of an occasion, no matter how good her cooking was.

Clay never worried about Coach coming over, but he was worried now, worried that Coach's thoughts might start to wander around while he was at their house; that he might say something or do something or even forget their names; that they'd see what Clay and Maddie had been seeing, even when they didn't have to look very hard.

Or that *he'd* say something to give things away.

But Coach was fine tonight, right through dessert. He was Coach, telling the same old stories, Clay's parents not thinking that was anything out of the ordinary, because he'd always told the same stories.

It was while they were having dessert that Coach invited Clay and his mom and dad to come with him, as his guests, to the Cowboys' reunion game on Thanksgiving up in Arlington. But as soon as he issued the invite, he started talking about how he understood they wouldn't be able to accept it.

"You probably got your plans all made," he said. "It's Thanksgiving, for criminy sakes, and I'm sure you got family things to do. But I just wanted you-all to know . . ."

That's as far as he got.

"We accept," Katherine Hollis said.

"Wait, I don't get a vote?" Ben Hollis said.

"See what I'm talking about," Coach said, jumping right back in. "I've imposed on you nice folks just by inviting you in the first place."

"Actually, Monty, that's not what I meant," Clay's dad said, grinning at Coach. "What I meant was that I never get the cast the first vote around here for a really good idea because some people"—he raised his eyebrows and nodding and smiling at his wife—"always manage to beat me to it."

"I'd stop digging now if I were you," Clay's mom said, smiling at her husband.

Clay said, "We can go to the game? Really?" He looked at his mom, then at his dad, then back at his mom, because he knew she was the one who called the shots on holidays.

His mom said, "We not only *can* go. We *are* going. And by the way, Monty? We *will* be with family when we do." She winked at Clay, who smiled.

Coach said he was supposed to get all his passes on Monday, and as soon as he had them, he'd come back over here and drop them off. He told Clay they were going to be like backstage passes at some big concert, and that he'd be able to go pretty much wherever he wanted to at AT&T Stadium.

"And I'll get to meet your teammates?" Clay said.

"Can't think of a reason in the world why not."

"Done deal!" he said.

After that they talked about the Stars and the game tomorrow and the season. And before Coach got up from the table and said his good-nights, he told Clay's parents how proud he was of their son and the way he'd battled through what he called "all that stuff."

"I taught your boy a lot about football, or so I like to tell myself," Coach Coop said. "But there's never a way to teach heart."

Clay said he'd walk Coach out. But when they got to the truck and it was just the two of them, Coach told Clay to put his head back and take a look up at the big Texas sky.

"Pick out one star and make a wish on it," Coach said.

Clay did.

"You, too," he said to Coach.

Coach smiled and then said, "Done deal."

They just stood there, looking up at the sky, until Coach said, "There's one thing I'll never forget, no matter what. And that's what you and your girl done for me this season."

Clay almost hugged him then, and told him how much he loved him. But he was afraid of embarrassing an old Cowboy like Monty Cooper. Instead he told Coach to hand over his phone, went to Waze, and showed him he was clicking on HOME.

"Feel like I'm home already," Coach said.

# THIRTY-TWO

**F**ROM THE TIME CLAY HAD first started caring about sports, it was his dad who'd always told him the same thing: That the very best thing about sports is that they were constantly surprising you. And now football had surprised Clay Hollis, as much as it possibly could.

All season long, even when he'd come up short and have to find a way to come back from that—and maybe surprise himself—the thing he kept thinking about the most and dreaming about the most was one big day: the day of the championship game, if the Stars could make it that far.

Now that day had come and gone. And the Stars had beaten the Bucs and become the champions of their league and even had their team picture published in the San Antonio *Express-News*. They had saved their best game until their last game. Clay had caught a touchdown pass. So had Will. Josh Bodeen had run for their last score. Bryce and the guys on D had pitched a shutout against Mac Sherrill and the Bucs' offense, sometimes pitching what looked to Clay on the sideline like a perfect game. It had ended up 20–0. Game over, season over. The trophy was theirs. The whole team went back to Clay's house for pizza and ice cream on the back lawn, November still feeling like summer in San Antonio.

None of that was the surprise for Clay.

The big surprise was that winning that game and winning that championship didn't feel as big as today did, Thanksgiving Day, at AT&T Stadium with Coach. Cowboys against the Redskins, and the reunion Coach and his teammates were set to have on the field at halftime, honoring the last Cowboys team to win the Super Bowl.

Coach's big day.

And to Clay, it felt bigger than anything, and not just because of the way they'd been allowed to walk all around AT&T, even getting to go inside the locker room when the players on the current Cowboys team were on the field warming up. Clay had even gotten to meet the owner of the team, Jerry Jones. And go stand with Coach Coop under the goalposts. Somehow the end zone here looked a whole lot bigger than the one at Holy Cross.

"Nice to be here with nobody trying to pick me off, or pick you off," David Guerrero said.

"Yeah," Clay said. "Middle of the field never looked so good."

Maddie was with them. So were Clay's parents. Clay's dad had driven everybody, including Coach, in the Hollises' SUV the day before. They'd all stayed at the Marriott that was close enough to AT&T that they could walk to the stadium. The night before, Coach had gone off to some big dinner with the '95 Cowboys and the rest of them ate dinner at the hotel. They were leaving early the next morning, both the Hollis family and the Guerrero family having decided to all eat dinner together on Friday, before just about everybody on the Stars was going to get together for a Turkey Bowl touch football game at Holy Cross.

Before they all went upstairs to watch most of the first half in a suite the Cowboys had provided for them, Coach spent most of the time grumping about how he'd never be able to find his way around this new place the way he could old Texas Stadium even if you'd blindfolded him there back in the day.

"Once I get upstairs, I'll probably need my phone just to find the *field*," he said.

"Don't worry, Coach," Maddie said. "It's like Clay and I keep telling you: You've got us."

Somehow Coach had worked it out with the people from the Cowboys running the halftime show that he could bring Clay and Maddie and David down with him. They couldn't go all the way out on the field, but could watch from the tunnel when Troy Aikman and Emmitt Smith and Michael Irvin and the rest of the old Cowboys took the field.

Them and Coach.

Before they did go upstairs, Coach took one last look up at the huge screen that stretched from one twenty-yard line to the other, what Clay had heard was the biggest screen of its kind in the whole world. Coach had seen it before, but still acted as if he couldn't believe his eyes.

"Everything looks better up there," he said. "Maybe I will, too."

"Impossible, Monty," Katherine Hollis said. "As far as I'm concerned, you've never looked better in your life."

Halfway through the second quarter, a young woman from the

Cowboys came into the suite and said that Monty's family had arrived.

"What are you talkin' about? My family's right here, already with me."

Coach looked at Clay, and Clay could see the confusion in his eyes. It was a different kind of confusion, though. Coach didn't seem lost or angry.

Clay smiled wide, and Maddie jumped up from her seat. She peeked behind the young woman who had entered the suite. Then they both moved aside.

There in the doorway was another woman, one Clay had only seen in photos before. She was tan, like she'd just stepped out of a postcard. And she was carrying a little boy.

Coach stood up. He almost looked afraid to smile, but he wasn't a person to let fear get in the way.

"Allie!"

Then everyone gave them room. There was a lot of hugging to make room for. A lot of time to make up for.

Soon after, the entire group was led down to the field. By the time they got down there, most of the other old Cowboys were there, too, awaiting the ceremony. Clay Hollis—the pro football history buff— recognized most of them even before they went into a big room near the Cowboys' locker room and changed into white Cowboys' home uniforms with their names and numbers on the back.

Before the game, Clay noticed it was Coach who was having trouble putting names to some of the faces. But it didn't take long for him to realize Clay could do it for him. So if he saw any hesitation from Coach when one of his teammates would head in his direction, Clay would whisper, "Moose Johnston." Or, "Larry Brown." Or, "Wade Wilson," who'd been a backup quarterback on that team.

Eventually, the half was over, and the Cowboys and Redskins came off the field; there was about a minute before the ceremony would begin. Clay felt as excited as if there were a minute left in a game he was playing.

Coach leaned down and said to Clay, "I still don't remember everybody."

Clay said, "You just be ready when they call your name and number, okay, hoss?"

"Okay," Coach said to him. Then he gave his grandson another kiss on the top of his head. "Best gift ever," Coach said to himself.

This, Clay knew, was the real end of his football season, one he knew he would remember as long as he lived. But he also knew that he wasn't ever going to forget all that he'd learned this season. Knew that he probably wouldn't ever love football quite the same way ever again because of all he *had* learned.

The public address announcer began to call the names now. Clay and Maddie had talked so much about this day because it was so important to Coach and because they knew that whatever was going on inside his head, there wasn't going to be a happy ending for him. All they knew, today, was that this ending, with *all* of his family, would have to do for now.

"Here we go," Coach said in a soft voice. "Just want to hear my number called one more time."

The announcements began and he wasn't Coach Coop right

then. He was number 19 of the 1995 Dallas Cowboys, down here with Troy and Emmitt and Deion Sanders and Richard Dent. And as exciting as *that* was for Clay, he couldn't believe how old some of them looked. How much some of them limped, the way Coach did. How slowly others moved around, almost as if they were afraid of falling. These were some of the biggest winners in the history of the Cowboys, but too many of them, Clay thought, looked as if they had lost some kind of fight with football. What had they each sacrificed to keep loving the game?

He wondered how many of them had forgotten more than just names.

Then he saw the smile on Coach's face. In the middle of AT&T Stadium. Larger than life, on the giant video screen, waving to the cheering crowd.

One more scrapbook day of his very own.

Author photo © Taylor Lupica

**MIKE LUPICA** has been called "the greatest sports writer for middle school readers." He is the author of multiple bestselling books, including *Heat, Travel Team, Million-Dollar Throw, The Underdogs, QB1, Fantasy League,* and *Fast Break.* As a sports columnist for New York's *Daily News* and a weekly member of ESPN's *The Sports Reporters,* which is televised nationally, he has proven that he can write for and speak to sports fans of all ages and stripes.